Praise for Javier Marías and

THE MAN OF FEELING

"A digressive narrative that moves back and forth in time. . . . There is nothing quite like it in fiction today." —*The New York Times Book Review*

"A book that reflects the torture of love the way arias reflect heartbreak."
—*The Washington Times*

"Marías's literary gamesmanship evokes verbal puzzlemakers like Borges, and his ingenious chessboard plots bring to mind the twentieth century's grand-master strategist, Vladimir Nabokov. Yet his style is uniquely his own, as are the discoveries he makes while rummaging around in the basement of the human heart."
—*Los Angeles Times*

Javier Marías

THE MAN OF FEELING

Javier Marías was born in Madrid in 1951. The recipient of numerous prizes, including the International IMPAC Dublin Literary Award and the Prix Femina Étranger, he has written thirteen novels, three story collections, and nineteen works of collected articles and essays. His books have been translated into forty-two languages, in fifty-two countries, and have sold more than seven and a half million copies throughout the world.

INTERNATIONAL

THE MAN
OF FEELING

A Novel

Javier Marías

Translated from the Spanish
by Margaret Jull Costa

Vintage International
Vintage Books
A Division of Random House LLC
New York

FIRST VINTAGE INTERNATIONAL EDITION, OCTOBER 2014

Translation copyright © 2003 by Margaret Jull Costa

All rights reserved. Published in the United States by Vintage Books, a division of Random House LLC, New York, and in Canada by Random House of Canada Limited, Toronto, Penguin Random House companies. Originally published in Spain as *El hombre sentimental* by Mercedes Casanovas Agencia Literaria, Barcelona, in 1986. Copyright © 1986 by Javier Marías. This translation originally published in the United Kingdom by the Harvill Press, London, in 2003.

Vintage is a registered trademark and Vintage International and colophon are trademarks of Random House LLC.

This is a work of fiction. Names, characters, places, and incidents either are the product of the author's imagination or are used fictitiously. Any resemblance to actual persons, living or dead, events, or locales is entirely coincidental.

The Cataloging-in-Publication Data is on file at the Library of Congress.

Vintage Trade Paperback ISBN: 978-0-8041-7259-2
eBook ISBN: 978-0-8041-7260-8

www.vintagebooks.com

Printed in the United States of America
10 9 8 7 6 5 4 3 2 1

For Daniella Pittarello
che magari still exists.

I think myself into love,
And I dream myself out of it.

William Hazlitt

I DON'T KNOW WHETHER I should tell you my dreams. They are old dreams, old-fashioned dreams, more suited to an adolescent than to a grown man. They are at once elaborate and precise, leisurely, but highly colored, like those dreamed by an over-imaginative but basically simple soul, a very orderly soul. They are dreams that become somewhat tedious after a while because the person dreaming them always wakes before the end, as if the dream impulse had worn itself out in the representation of all those details and lost interest in the final result, as if dreaming were the only truly ideal and aimless activity left. So I do not know how my dreams end, and it might be inconsiderate of me to tell you about them, knowing that I can offer neither conclusion nor lesson. But they strike me as both inventive and vivid. The only thing I can say in my defense is that I am writing out of the particular form of timelessness—the place of my eternity—that has chosen me.

However, what I dreamed this morning, when it was already light, is something that really happened and that happened to me when I was slightly younger, or less old than I am now, and which is not yet over.

Four years ago, because of my work (I am a professional singer) and just before I made a miraculous recovery from my fear of flying, I made numerous journeys by train over a fairly short space of time, some six weeks in total. That brief but continuous period of traveling took me through the western part of our continent, and it was on the penultimate of these trips (from Edinburgh to London, from London to Paris, and from Paris to Madrid in a day and a night) that I saw for the first time the three faces I dreamed about this morning, which are the same faces that have occupied part of my imagination, much of my memory, and my whole life (respectively) from then up until now, that is, for four years.

The truth is that it took me a while to notice them, as if something were warning me or as if, unwittingly, I wanted to delay the danger and the happiness involved in noticing them (but I'm afraid this idea belongs more to my dream than to actual reality). I had been reading the pompous memoirs of an Austrian writer, but was finding them intensely irritating (in fact, that morning they were really getting on my nerves), and at one point I closed the book and, contrary to my habit when I travel by train and I am not talking or reading or reviewing my repertoire or reliving past failures and successes, I did not look "directly" at the landscape, but at my fellow passengers. The woman was asleep, but the two men were awake.

However, the first man, sitting immediately opposite me, was looking at the landscape, his large head of greying curls turned to his right, and one unusually small hand—so small it did not seem possible that it could belong to any real human body—slowly stroking his cheek. I could only see his features in profile, but considering the essential ambiguity of his age—for his was one of those mysterious physiques which gives the impression that it is resisting the pressures of time rather better than most, as if the threat of sudden death and the hope of remaining fixed forever with its image unscathed were compensation enough for the effort involved—he appeared somewhat more than mature by virtue both of the abundant frosted vegetation that crowned his head and of the two fissures—like woody incisions in his burnished skin—which, positioned on either side of a weak, and at first sight, inexpressive mouth, gave one the impression, nonetheless, of a person quite prepared to smile for decades whether it was appropriate to do so or not. At that moment of his ageless life he struck one as a placid sort, a slight man with plenty of money, wearing a pair of elegant trousers—if somewhat worn and just a touch too short, one could almost see his shins—and a brand new jacket made of a fabric that combined rather too many colors. A man who had come into money late in life, I thought; perhaps the owner of a medium-sized business, someone independent but hard-working. Since I could not see his eyes, which were turned towards the outside world, I could not have said if he was a lively or a sombre individual (although he was very perfumed, suggesting a faded but as yet unvanquished coquetry). At any rate, he was looking with extraordinary attentiveness, one might almost say loquacity, as if he were witnessing the instantaneous creation of a drawing or as if what was there before his eyes were water or even fire, from which it is sometimes so hard to avert one's gaze. But landscape is never dramatic, not like the creation of a drawing, not like restless water or tentative fire, and that is why watching a landscape brings repose to the weary and bores those who never weary. Despite my strong build and a constitution about which I cannot complain, bearing in mind that my profession requires it to be made of iron, I often get extremely weary, which is why I too opted for looking at the landscape, only "indirectly," through the invisible eyes of the man with the small hands, elegant trousers, and extravagant jacket. But since it was growing dark, I could see almost nothing—only bas-reliefs—and I thought that perhaps the man was looking at himself in the glass. Indeed, only a few minutes later, when the light gently surrendered after the brief, hesitant glow of a northern sunset, I saw him duplicated, divided, repeated, almost as clearly in the glass of the window as in reality. I decided that the man was indeed studying his own face, he was looking at himself.

The second man, sitting diagonally opposite me, stared immutably ahead. He had one of those faces the mere contemplation of which brings unease to the soul of someone for whom the road ahead is still unclear or, to put it another way, who still depends on his own efforts. His presumably premature baldness had done nothing to impair his satisfaction or his belief in his own thirst for power, nor had it tempered—or even clouded—the chilling expression in his eyes, eyes accustomed to skim rapidly over the things of the world—accustomed to being flattered by the things of the world—and which were the color of cognac. Any insecurity of his own had allowed itself only the tribute of a neat, black moustache with which to disguise his plebeian features and to offset somewhat the incipient plumpness—which, to eyes in thrall to him, might still have passed for robustness—of head, neck and chest, the last of which tended to convexity. This man was a tycoon, a man of ambition, a politician, an exploiter, and his clothes, especially the shiny jacket and the tie and tie pin, seemed to have come from across the ocean, or were some refined European concession to a style considered elegant abroad. He must have been some ten years older than me, but the slight tic immediately apparent in the merest hint of a smile that his thick lips now and then silently rehearsed—like someone changing position or crossing and uncrossing his legs, nothing more—made me think that there must also be a touch of the child in this arrogant man's makeup, which, together with his robust physique, would make those who saw that smile react with a mixture of derision and terror, and a few drops of irrational compassion. Maybe this was the only thing lacking in his life: that his wishes should be understood and carried out without him making them known. Though confident of getting his own way, he might perhaps be obliged to resort again and again to tricks, threats, insults, fits. But maybe only to amuse himself, in order occasionally to test out his talents as an actor and to maintain flexibility, or perhaps in order to hone his subjugating skills, for, as I well know, the most effective and long-lasting subjugations are based on pretence or, indeed, on something that has never existed. This man who, in my dream, I judged from the start to be as cowardly as he was tyrannical, did not look at me—nor did the other man—not even once, not as far as I could tell, not, at least, while I was looking at him. This man about whom I now know far too much, as I say, stared impassively ahead, as if written across the empty seat opposite—which he almost certainly did not see—was a detailed account of a future already known to him and which he was merely verifying.

While this exploitative individual revealed his whole face, and the other somewhat mysterious fellow only his profile, the woman who was sitting between them, and with whom the men may or may not have been traveling, for the moment lacked any face. Her head was back, but her face was covered by her straight, brown hair, deliberately thrown forward, perhaps to protect her shallow train-bound sleep from the light, perhaps, too, so as not to offer up, gratis, the image of intimacy and abandon of which she herself would be unaware, her sleeping, lifeless image. She had her legs crossed, and her low-heeled winter boots revealed the upper part of her calf, which went on to become a knee, where the slight sheen of her tights intensified, and ended at the frontiers of a black skirt apparently made of suede. Her whole figure, deprived of its face, gave an impression of perfection, fixity, completion and acceptance, as if there were no room in her for change, emendation or denial—like the days that are ended, like legends, like the liturgy of established religions, like the paintings from centuries past that no one would dare to touch. Her hands, resting in her lap, lay one on top of the other, the right hand with the palm open, the left hand—hanging down—half-closed. But the thumb of that hand—which had long, rather gnarled fingers, like those of someone tempted to bid a premature farewell to youth—made the slight, involuntary, spasmodic movements of someone who has fallen asleep despite herself. She was wearing an anachronistic pearl necklace; she was wearing a red stole around her neck; she was wearing a double silver ring on her middle finger. Her hair, arranged with a single, much-practiced toss of the head, did not even allow one to build up an image of the whole face from a single feature, falling as densely as an opaque veil. That is why I spent so much time studying her hands. Apart from the occasional movement of her thumb, there was something else that attracted my attention: not so much her nails—firm, off-white, manicured—but the surrounding skin, which looked terribly bitten or burned, so much so that the skin on her index fingers—because they were the worst affected—was virtually non-existent, indeed one might have doubted it had ever existed at all. The skin around these nails had suffered some serious eruption that had left behind an ugly red color, as if the skin were inflamed or raw. I thought that if it was the latter (I could not take a closer look), then it was the work not so much of the unseen incisors of the sleeping woman and of the child she had once been, as of time itself, for atrophy—for that was what it seemed to be—requires not only lack of use and activity, not only systematic suppression, but also that most temporal of all things and the thing that distracts all other things from their temporal nature: habit (or its ever-tardy daughter, the law, who is also the first to say that habit's time is nearly up and to announce an end to distraction). I was just beginning to get slightly carried away by these thoughts about a subject of which I understand nothing and, in fact, know nothing, when a sudden sideways jolt of the train made that glossy, straight, brown hair momentarily uncover the face it had been guarding. The face did not wake up, and only a few seconds later everything returned to its original position, but from the full, tight, tense lips, from the tight, tense eyelids with their tracery of tiny reddish veins (the eyes were closed and still unseen), I saw that the sleeping woman was, how can I put it, afflicted. Perhaps I saw that she was afflicted by a kind of melancholy dissolution.

"I DON'T WANT TO DIE LIKE A FOOL," I said to this woman shortly afterwards, in a hotel room that was dark, cramped and of a squalor I did not at the time notice, with bare walls and bedspreads that were grey or possibly just forlorn or simply forgotten in a heap on the floor, fitted with a clean but discolored carpet, and on which there was barely space enough to walk, with two half-unpacked suitcases taking up the space between bed and bathroom, so empty and so white that two toothbrushes—dark red and green—placed in one glass, whose cellophane wrapping had disappeared though we never knew precisely when or who had made it disappear, drew the gaze the way a hand is drawn to a dagger or iron to a magnet, so much so that when one of those toothbrushes was missing on the last night I was there, the ceramic surfaces and the tiles on the floor and walls were all tinged with the red of the remaining toothbrush, and that color even appropriated the black of the toilet bag which I left on the glass shelf so that her departure would be marked by some change or some sign of mourning in that bathroom, so empty and so white, which could be reached only by climbing over the half-unpacked suitcases and the forgotten bedspreads in a heap on the floor when, shortly afterwards, in a hotel bedroom, I said to that same woman: "I don't want to die like a fool, and since, one day or another, I will have no choice but to die, I want above all to take good care, while I can, of the one thing that is certain and irremediable, but I want especially to take care of the manner of my death because the manner is not quite so certain and irremediable. It is the manner of our death that we should take good care of, and in order to do so, we should take good care of our life, because it is that which, although nothing in itself once it ceases or is replaced, is the one thing which, nevertheless, will tell us if, in the end, we died a fool's death or a perfectly acceptable death. You are my life and my love and my life's knowledge, and because you are my life, I do not want to have anyone else but you by my side when I die. But I do not want you to rush to my deathbed when you learn that I am dying, nor to come to my funeral to say goodbye when I can no longer see you or smell you or kiss your face, nor even that you should agree, or want, to accompany me in my last years simply because the two of us have survived our respective and pitiful or separate lives, that isn't enough. What I want there to be at the hour of my death is the incarnation of my life—what that life has been—and in order for you to have been that too, you must have lived by my side from now until that final moment. I could not bear it if at that moment you were only a memory or a confused figure belonging to a vague and distant time which is this clear time that we are living now, because it is memory and distant time and confusion that I most detest and which I have always tried to diminish and reject and bury as soon as they began to form, as soon as each dear, noble present moment ceased to be present and became the past, and was vanquished by what I can only call its own impatient posterity, its not-nowness. That is why you must not leave now, because if you leave now, you will take from me not only my life and my love and my life's knowledge, but also the chosen manner of my death."

I can still remember perfectly how she listened to me as she lay on the bed in that hotel bedroom: she was barefoot but still dressed, leaning on her elbows and with her legs bent; her grey skirt had ridden up slightly to reveal part of her thigh; her straight, glossy brown hair was tilted away from me; and her sweet, grave, ironic gaze was so intent on my incessant lips that it made me feel as if I were only my lips, and that my lips were solely responsible for creating whatever emerged from them.

"And what if I die first?"

"Anything is possible," I replied at once. But I think I did so in order to disguise or to postpone a little (I did it to gain time) the only other normal and admissible answer that immediately followed, the one she was waiting for, as would any mortal lying as she was, at that moment, on that bed: "But your death would also be mine." "But your death would also be mine," I said to this same woman and, just as happens in opera, I repeated these same words several times in this morning's dream.

MY PROFESSION OFTEN OBLIGES ME to lead a very solitary life in the great capitals of the world, and four years ago, Madrid, the city in which I spent much of my childhood and much of my adolescence, was no exception. Indeed, after a long period without visiting it, few cities I have been to on my numerous trips abroad have seemed to me sadder or more solitary. More even than English cities, which are the worst in the world, the most miserable and the most hostile; more even than those of East Germany, which are so disciplined and so deadened that to walk down the street whistling has a cataclysmic effect; more even than those of Switzerland, which are at least clean and quiet and give free rein to the imagination precisely because they say nothing.

Madrid, on the other hand, seems in a hurry to say everything, as if it were aware that the only way it can win over the traveler is through unchecked noise and vehemence. It does not, therefore, allow for any long-term expectations, any reticence or reserve, nor does it allow the visitor (not to mention the perpetually harassed resident) the smallest imaginative or imaginary hope that anything more might exist—hidden, unexpressed, omitted or merely contingent—than what is brazenly offered to him as soon as he steps out along its dirty, suffocating streets. Madrid is rustic and talkative and lacks all mystery, and there is nothing so sad or so solitary as a city with no apparent enigma or even the appearance of an enigma, there is nothing so dissuasive, nothing so oppressive to a visitor. I, both in my dream and four years ago, was a visitor to this city despite having lived in it and in its environs when I was no more than a child and entirely dependent on my godfather, who took me in and moved me there from Barcelona when my mother died. (I was for many years what is known as a poor relation: I was quite literally that, and it was then that I lived in Madrid. On the other hand, at the time, four years ago, I had long since ceased to be a poor relation and was making a good living, but, given my prolonged absence and the minimal contact I had had with my former benefactor since my emancipation, I was just as much a visitor to Madrid as I had been to Venice and Milan and Edinburgh a few weeks earlier.)

As I said, I was taken there and am still taken to all these cities by my profession, which, contrary to popular belief, is one of the saddest and most solitary of professions—people only ever see us on stage, on record covers, on posters and in the occasional televised gala performance: that is, always in full make-up. The truth is that, in essence, we are not so very different from traveling salesmen, except, of course, that profession is slowly dying out and is in danger of disappearing altogether, doubtless because the people in charge of large companies, though, on the whole, highly pragmatic individuals not known for their humanitarianism, have realized that no one can lead such a hard, disparate life. I have known traveling salesmen who have ended up in mental hospitals, or have murdered a would-be customer, or committed suicide in a luxury hotel, knowing that their unusual excesses (indoor swimming pool, sauna, massages, cocktails, but, above all, the dry-cleaning bill) would be vainly deducted from a posthumous salary that they had taken good care to overspend and which no one would notice anyway. At least they would die with their suit pressed.

Opera singers always stay in luxury hotels and our excesses are neither unusual nor excessive, but rather the norm and what is required, yet our life in the city where we have come to work is not so very different from that of a traveling salesman. In every hotel in which I have stayed—in every hotel, therefore, in which there was a singer—there was at least one traveling salesman who, during my sojourn, slashed his wrists in a bubble bath or ruthlessly knifed a bellboy, performed a striptease in the foyer, set fire to a carpet, used the fire extinguisher to smash the mirrors in his luxury suite or, in the elevator, fondled the wife of a member of some government. And before or after such an outburst, I have always identified with some detail, some characteristic, some gesture of utter weariness which I had noticed in the salesman when we coincided in the elevator late at night, tie dishevelled and eyes docile; in a shared, sideways glance of patience and defeat; in the discreet way we smoothed our hair or mopped our brow with a handkerchief; in the unoriginal manner of their suicide. I have on occasion found myself in the company of just such a moribund traveling salesman in the hotel bar, perched on stools a few yards apart, letting another already dead hour pass in that area which is always the first place you seek out as soon as you move in, so as to have a third refuge or support (the first is your room, the foyer is the second) to protect us or guard us from having to go straight out into the world, into the new, unknown and unknowing city, where nothing needs us and where we are ignored by everything. On such occasions, however, if the salesman has happened to find out what or who I am, he has not regarded me as I have him, as an equal or as a fellow sufferer, but with envy and resentment. Indeed, even if they didn't find out: my clothes are better, my self-confidence more apparent, my way of holding my glass more nonchalant, my legs always loosely crossed, the handkerchief with which I dab my forehead is clean and neatly folded and possibly colorful, while his is crumpled and dirty and invariably white; and his brow more furrowed. The difference has less to do with the degree of fame (non-existent in his case) or an awareness of the prestige to be gained by the exercise of our respective professions than with our familiarity with a certain type of terrain: thus while the traveling salesman is only staying in a luxury hotel out of extreme despair and cannot but feel himself to be an intruder—a poor relation whose admittance there is an exception, for there he will give full rein to his disquiet or else celebrate his own death—I am an artist and a man of the world and I am there because of my work, my despair is either latent or merely in the incubating stage, and I cannot see my own presence in that place as a transgression or an abuse of trust or even as a challenge, but rather as merely routine; to me, my presence there does not, as it does for him, have either a symbolic meaning or the character of an ultimatum. It is in no way a cry for help, as it is in his case. Nor does it portend anything. However, this has not prevented me from occasionally seeing in the destroyed or potentially self-destroying traveling salesman a shadow or an anticipation of what awaits me. He is at the end of a sad, solitary life, while the opera singer has still not reached the end of his for the simple reason that he is never quite as convinced as the traveling salesman that this life of his is, in fact, sad and solitary. The greasepaint makes him less clear-sighted.

But, notwithstanding all these differences, I say again that life in the big cities is very similar for both professions. We opera singers arrive in a place: we are met at the hotel (although not always, and, of course, never at the airport or the station) and we are mildly fêted on the first night by the organizers (that is, by the impresarios, by the contracting party who *pretend* to have invited us). All the honors and almost all the niceties end there, because from the next day onwards we begin a period of one or two or even three weeks during which we have strict obligations to fulfill, and all we do is rehearse, snack, rehearse and sleep, barely departing from the route taken between hotel and rehearsal hall or, if making a recording, the studio. Bearing in mind that impresarios always judge that they are doing us a great favor by arranging for the two places to be close to each other, the routes we take through the cities we visit are often only a few hundred yards long (unless the existence of an old friend in the locality causes us to deviate or if, out of rebelliousness or curiosity, we propose other routes). I am not a conformist, but, rather, an exception, for I have colleagues for whom an immense city with thousands of inhabitants consists of one or two or three streets which they travel only on foot. When you go to a place to work, you don't feel like visiting it; on the contrary, what we opera singers try to do is forget that we are in a different place from the one we've just been to, in the hope that we will avoid a geographical (as well as, in our case, linguistic) schizophrenia, which could lead us to the same crazed, criminal or suicidal end as that of so many traveling salesmen. To the great good fortune of most of us singers, one luxury hotel is always much like any other luxury hotel, and one recording studio or rehearsal hall is much like any other recording studio or rehearsal hall, and, ultimately, one cheering, applauding audience is much like any other audience who respond in more or less the same way, so much so that many of my colleagues manage to persuade themselves—intermittently—that every time they leave home and go off to work in another country or another town, the country or town in question does not vary, but is always the same. By means of this fiction, they try to convince themselves that they are not completely abnormal, itinerant people, that they are no different, for example, from university teachers who live in a capital city but teach in a provincial town, cramming all their classes into two days, or soccer players, who are only away on Saturdays and Sundays (and international soccer players on occasional Wednesdays), but that they are, on the other hand, quite different from professional golfers and lecturers, tennis champions, bullfighters during the season, and traveling salesmen.

When we stay in cities, therefore, we generally try—and even if we didn't, things couldn't easily be different—to deal only with those in our own profession: the other performers in the opera in which we are going to appear, the members of the chorus (if there is one), the extras, and the orchestra, all of whom are sufficiently much of a muchness everywhere for them likewise not to underline for us the unfortunate and troubling fact that we find ourselves in a place which is not at all the same place we were in a few days ago or even a few weeks or months or years ago. But the problem with carrying this illusion through to its logical consequences lies in the fact that, were the place really the same on all occasions (as we try to pretend in our conscious mind), we would surely, in that case, have made friends there, and would feel as if it were our second home; more than that, we would actually *have* a second home there and would not be staying in a hotel. But since this is not the case, our lives, despite all the efforts of our imagination and all the conveniences, despite all the money we earn, despite the bouquets, the applause, the ovations and the acclaim, are ultimately just like those of traveling salesmen—who, however, are becoming extinct—at least during each of our sad and solitary sojourns in the great capitals of the world. And our lives are one long sojourn.

But I am not like most singers. After the long, unsatisfactory and often irritating rehearsals, the last thing I want is the company of my colleagues and of the members of the orchestra (first violin and conductor included), not just because staying with them is in many ways an unconscious prolongation of work, but because you really cannot talk to them about anything else but work or about the world surrounding work, which means music or the world of music, and I have never seen the point of talking about music, it has always struck me as either exhausting and arid or frustrating and stupid. Either you talk about the technical aspects, which is exhausting and arid, or you talk in sentimental terms, which is just frustrating and stupid, mere chatter. Indeed, music aside, my colleagues' conversation is no better than that of office workers, because they have the souls of office workers. Besides, unlike most of them, I enjoy the feeling that I am in a new and unfamiliar city; going into public places and being aware that the people there speak a language I know only imperfectly or not at all; studying the clothes and hats (though nowadays one sees fewer of the latter) that the good citizens choose to wear in the street; finding out if shops are full or empty during office hours; seeing how the news is treated in the newspapers; looking at certain examples of domestic architecture that one can only find in that particular part of the world; noting the typefaces that predominate in shop signs (and reading these like a savage, understanding nothing); scrutinizing the faces in the metro and on the busses which I frequent for that very reason; picking out particular faces and wondering whether I might or might not meet them elsewhere; deliberately getting lost in parts of the city where I have already learned to find my way, that is, with map in hand if I need it; observing the inimitable passing of each languishing day at each point on the globe and the uncertain and variable instant when the lights are lit; setting foot in places where our feet leave no trace, on the luminous asphalt of the morning or on some dusty, ancient stone pavement illuminated by a single street lamp as evening falls; visiting bars full of indistinguishable, blithely insignificant murmurings that cover and erase everything; mingling with the people in the white streets of the south or in the grey avenues of the north at the declining hour when people are going out for a stroll or coming home from work, that brief respite; seeing how the women go out in the evening or perhaps at night, all dressed up, and seeing the cars in their many colors waiting for them; imagining the parties they are going to; wasting time. And in each city I visit I would like to meet people, to meet those smartly dressed women, who are perhaps climbing into their glossy, impeccable cars to drive to the opera to hear León de Nápoles: to go and see me.

Now that I am reasonably famous, because I appear now and then on the televisions of the world, I usually get to know someone or other, albeit superficially, wherever I go; such people, however, are nearly always admirers, whose questions and sameness bore me. But four years ago, when I still had to make do with roles like Spoletta, Trabuco, Dancaïro and even Monostatos (it's a good role, but I hated having to make myself up like a bald negro), I found it impossible to form any kind of relationship with the inhabitants of those cities, who would merely look at me the way one looks at an advertisement for a performance in a foreign newspaper which one reads at home. That is why, despite my inclinations, curiosity and non-conformity, I would often have to give in and lead the same kind of monotonous, lax and rather unimaginative life led by other singers. I found it exasperating not being able to blend in with the local population except on a purely physical and incidental level (sharing the same space or, at most, rubbing shoulders with them in various forms of public transport), not being able to take part in the deals and the desires being cooked up right there in front of me, nor in the determined, almost mechanical movements—denoting an objective, a plan, a job, haste—of the passers-by and the drivers who were continually passing before my gaze wherever I was in the city and whenever I chose to go on one of my rambles. It irritated me not to be one of them; it irritated me not being able to share their souls. Even the hotel foyer, by definition plagued with strangers, with people—like me—who were just passing through, filled me with infinite unease and envy: everyone, even those who clearly are just waiting, resting or killing time, gives the impression that they know exactly what they want, they all seem so busy, so determined, as if they were just about to set off to some place whose existence takes on real meaning because it is expecting them, so absorbed are they in their present or imminent or dreamed-of or planned activities that my awareness of my own dead hours used to depress me immensely, so much so that during my stays in hotels, I came to enjoy only the moment in the morning when I would stride across the foyer carrying a file full of scores and notes in order to step out into the street and head for the rehearsal hall, plus the few minutes that it took me to get there: the only moment in the day when my appearance and my gait and my gestures could become assimilated with those of everyone else, the only moment when I too, like those fortunate settled citizens, was obliged to direct my feet, I had no other option, towards a particular, pre-established place, a place—even more importantly—arranged beforehand by members (the opera impresarios) of that mysterious and elusive community. En route I would walk quickly and determinedly, head up and eyes front, stopping only for the traffic lights, not noticing faces or buildings, immersed in the self-absorbed, anonymous, ever-changing morning flood of people, knowing—for once—where I was going and where I had to go. I really savored that moment, as brief as it was coveted, in which I could at last pass among the crowd as one of them and, consequently, feel no desire to know anyone I did not already know. For one takes it for granted that someone who lives in a city all the time has—for good or ill, satisfactorily or unsatisfactorily—filled his quota of acquaintances.

In my leisure time, however, once I had returned to the hotel and, above all, when, after rehearsals, I had already spent a long time wandering fruitlessly through the city—always feeling an integral part of what in the great capitals of the world is known as the floating population—the only possibility remaining to me of meeting someone, even another foreigner or visitor like myself, was in the foyer or bar of the hotel, where, as I have said, the only person generally available and eager to strike up some sort of conversation (with no monetary or sexual interest involved, for, with the odd exception, these are not the best conduits to a sharing of souls) was the traveling salesman who, on those particular dates, has decided to lodge in that particular luxury hotel in order to prove fleetingly that, even far from home and among those who travel, there exist other lives in which suits are always pressed, and thus be confirmed in his utter despair and reaffirmed in his rebellion or death.

BUT NOT ALL OF THIS WAS IN MY morning dream, or at least not in such an orderly fashion as I am relating it now, but the dream was imbued with all the feelings

I've described, feelings that, were just as oppressively present in what had once been my own city, Madrid, when I arrived there four years ago to play what, up until then, had been one of my most important roles, that of Cassio in Verdi's *Otello*. I remember spending two whole days in the grip of these extremely unpleasant feelings, which were made all the worse in Madrid because there the buildings constituted neither novelty nor rediscovery, and contemplation of them did not, therefore, provide me with much distraction during my walks around the city, and above all because, although I felt like a visitor, I knew that I wasn't a visitor, at least not strictly speaking, and I was afraid that what I most desired in other cities might actually happen: that, given my inevitable recollection of the place, given my appearance—possibly, who knows, my actual features— given my lack of accent in my own language, I might be taken for a native or a resident. Everything was at the same time strangely familiar and alien, intimate and reprehensible, from the ridiculous, affected gait of the inhabitants to the grimy, suffocating atmosphere in nearly all the streets, from the ill-disciplined traffic— directed by delinquents—always full of taxis (although these were now mostly white not black) to the bars which were inexplicably packed at the most unseemly hours, from the constant gabble and the brusque manners to the anachronistic façades of the cinemas with their vast billboards, and the omnipresent garbage trucks. All of it abominable and utterly typical.

Perhaps it was the overwhelming sense of ambivalence in my contact with the city as a whole that made me hesitate rather longer than usual on my third night in the hotel bar—where at least the degree of familiarity and strangeness was within the habitual bounds of all capital cities—over whether the other man sitting there, while I was sipping a glass of hot milk before going to bed, the two of us separated by several feet of empty bar, looked more familiar to me than usual because his was a face from my remote Madrid past and who—for example—had just happened to arrange to meet someone there, or because he combined every one of the most common characteristics of traveling salesmen on their way to the four final truths: the bright, shining eyes of someone who has suddenly lost all scruples or is delaying the advent of a unique experience the nature of which he alone will decide; the slightly worn clothes which, at first sight, look new: rehabilitated too suddenly and too soon; a need to drink which one senses is quite recent and which is comparable only to the need felt by certain Nordic types on some festive eve or to that felt by Americans when they set themselves down at a bar, an act, it seems, indissolubly linked in their imaginations to the ingesting of alcohol as both process and goal; an undisguised predisposition to dialogue which, however, has nothing to do with the verbal diarrhea of certain drunks—for traveling salesmen, however drunk, keep a cautious grasp on their prudence until the very moment when they explode, for fear of being unmasked prematurely—and which is only evident in the impatient glances they give the disdainful barman or the other customers; the sagging or, at best, loose-fitting socks (something about which the dry-cleaner can do nothing); the position of their hands, often folded and resting on the table or the bar in a gesture of uncertainty—a remnant of prayers, which may or may not be answered—a gesture in which I too have sometimes found momentary relief from my latent despair. It was this man's hands—tiny hands like those emerging from frilled cuffs in paintings or from eighteenth-century costumes—which, after a few involuntary sideways glances on my part and much racking of my memory, allowed me to identify him as the individual who had sat opposite me on the train four or five days before. I had not immediately recognized him because, despite his highly unusual appearance, the first time I saw him I had been deprived of the two things which I could now observe unimpeded, first, while he kept shooting me insistent looks and, subsequently, when he finally turned and addressed me in an act of recognition that seemed almost simultaneous with my own, and which were, in fact, the most striking thing about him (more even than his perverse jacket, more than his huge head, more than his presumptuous perfume): his indisputably bulging eyes and the large expanse of protuberant gum that his brief and cordial smile instantly revealed.

"You," he said, pointing at my chin with a movement of his little finger that seemed to me overly intimate in a stranger, "you were on the same train as us a few days ago, weren't you?" And without giving me time either to reply or to agree, he added: "Don't you remember me?"

These two sentences, exactly as they were spoken, albeit with more emphasis on the word *us*, were repeated over and over in this morning's dream, while I watched—although it was, I think, in black and white—the pleased and candid smile on the face of that man, Dato, who was holding an almost empty glass of whisky in one hand, while with the other he was still pointing at my chin with the easy satisfaction of someone who finally sees before him the person for whom he has long been waiting. Yes, I remembered him. I remembered him. I do not know why the selective memory of dreams is so different from that of our conscious senses, but I cannot believe in those vengeful explanations according to which the things that the latter suppresses resurface, in various guises, in the former. Such a belief, I feel, contains an excessively religious element, a vague idea of reparation in which I cannot help but see traces of such things as the presence of evil, turning a blind eye, the oppression of the just, the struggle between opposites, the truth waiting to be revealed and the idea that there is a part of us which is in closer contact with the divinities than our own direct perceptions. And that is why I am more inclined to believe that the frequent slowing down of time in dreams provides a civilized, conventional breathing space of a dramatic or narrative or rhythmic nature, like the end of a chapter or an interval in a play, like a post-prandial cigarette or the minutes spent leafing through the newspaper before getting down to work, the pause before reading a long-feared letter or that last glance in the mirror before going out for the night. Or perhaps it is merely hesitation, for dream truth and dream reasoning are not always as straightforward as they are made out to be. Some dreams contain as much vacillation, backsliding, and dead time, as one finds in the broad light of day. Occasionally it may be necessary to play for time in order to channel that dead time, that is, it may be necessary deliberately to kill time. I am not so very far removed from the beliefs of certain ancients and, like them, apart from any premonitions and warnings that we give to ourselves, I see in dreams intuitions and explanations that are not in the least at odds with our alert consciousness, but which are, in fact, explicit comments about the world—however metaphorical: there is no contradiction in that—about the same and only world that accommodates the daylight world, regardless of how alien the nocturnal realm may seem to us in the morning. For example, I have dreamed that I was singing Wagner, something I will never sing or, rather, should not sing because my voice isn't suited to it and I lack the necessary training. However, I *could* sing Wagner in the broad light of day if I made myself; more than that, in the broad light of day, I can remember, perfectly, whole Wagnerian roles which I would not even attempt to hum to myself while I was shaving; but I *can* think them, even though I am not in a position to actually reproduce them, as, indeed, could any person who, though not a singer, has a memory, as indeed could a traveling salesman if he knew the roles. I do this with my waking senses, I sing and don't sing just as I do and don't sing when I dream I am singing Wagner. And last night I dreamed about what happened to me four years ago in the real world, if such a term serves any purpose or can usefully be contrasted with anything else. Of course there were differences, because although the facts and my vision of the story all correspond, I dreamed what happened in another order, in another tempo and with time apportioned and divided differently, in a concentrated, selective manner and—this is the decisive and incongruous part—knowing beforehand what had happened, knowing, for example, Dato's name, character and subsequent behavior before our first meeting took place in my dream. The strange thing is that, while in my mind there was synthesis, in my dream there was progression. It is true, on the other hand, that while I was dreaming, I could not know if my dream would depart at a given moment from what happened four years ago or if it would keep close to it until the end, as proved to be the case and as I now know and can say as the morning advances. But it is also true that now I do not know to what extent I am recounting what actually happened and to what extent I am describing what happened in my dream version of events, even though both things seem to me to be one and the same. I once read in a book by a German writer that people who choose not to eat breakfast are trying to avoid contact with the day so as not to enter fully into it because it is only through that second awakening, that of the stomach, that you can entirely leave behind you the darkness and the nocturnal realm, and it is only once you have arrived safe and sound on the other shore that you can allow yourself to recount what you dreamed without bringing down calamities upon yourself, since, if you do so before you have broken your fast, you are still under the sway of the dream and you betray it with your words, thus exposing yourself to its vengeance. And you tell it as if you were still asleep. Beneath its pretended intention of taking the dream very seriously indeed, this idea, which has unmistakably popular origins, conceals—as do those bandied about by psychiatrists, psychologists, psychoanalysts, psychotherapists and all the other usurpers of the word "psyche"—an infinite scorn for the dream, because it is based on the assumption that there are two separate worlds, that of dreaming and that of waking, or, even worse, two hostile, contrary worlds, fearful of each other, ready to hide their wealth and knowledge, and never to share them or combine them except through the violent capture, forced conversion, and invasive interpretation of one of the territories, with the peculiarity that the only world that feels this yearning for submission, the only one that achieves this spirit of conquest, is the diurnal world. But what prompted me to this confession is that, while I do not accept such an idea, I have chosen, just in case, not to have any breakfast this morning, in the hope that I will be able to tell both what happened and the dream of what happened, by dint of not distinguishing between them. That is why I have still not eaten anything, and who knows when I will.

AND YET I FIND MYSELF RESISTING telling you everything. A poor tenor who is afraid of his own story and of his own dreams, as if using words instead of lyrics, words that have not been dictated, invented phrases rather than repetitive written texts, learned, and memorized, had paralyzed his powerful voice, which up until now has only known the recitative style. I find it hard to speak without a libretto.

I was not an entirely free man then, and what I do not know and what I fear I will never know is why I lied about this to Dato that night in the hotel bar, when he enquired about my marital status. It wasn't one of his first questions, but it makes no difference: I could not have imagined then what he was going to propose without actually saying that he was proposing something. And if I had told the truth, he might not have proposed anything.

"Ah, so you're a singer. I should have guessed as much from that great chest of yours, and those shoulders, those pectorals, that virile appearance; you know, you look exactly as everyone imagines a singer should look. Now I don't know much about music, but I love it, all of it, I don't mind what it is, I can happily listen to music whatever I'm doing, really, anywhere, any time. Yours must be a fascinating life."

Up until the moment when I lied about my situation, I was telling him the truth, although, from the start, I found Dato's manner very hard to take and his comments utterly trivial, so much so that just as I was about to respond, I was seriously considering whether it was worth getting involved in a boring conversation of a kind I'd had thousands of times before and which was (as can be seen) tinged with the inevitable impertinence of the ignorant, and all for the sake of a little company in what had once been my own city. But, despite his manner and his opening remarks, the truth is there was something intriguing about the fellow (whom I no longer believed to be a traveling salesman: he was too relaxed, his voice and his gestures too languid, his clothes, on closer inspection, too expensive) and, at the same time, too, there was something about him that invited confidence. For all his worldly tone, his appearance and his expression still struck me as unreal or perhaps too real, like a Daumier caricature. He smiled constantly and easily, revealing those great, bulging gums that seemed about to burst at any moment, and gestured animatedly with his miniature hands.

"Well, I don't know about fascinating. It's varied and interesting, and all the moving around certainly keeps you on your toes. But, although it might not seem like it, it's a pretty hard, solitary existence. All that traveling is very unsettling." And I spoke to him briefly (though vehemently) about my sorrows and my discontents, about my partial or latent despair, and then asked him the obligatory question: "And what do you do?"

As I said earlier, by then, indeed as soon as I recognized him as being the same man who had been staring so intently out of the train window, I had rejected the idea of him being a traveling salesman, but apart from what I had thought at the time (without much conviction or insight, that he owned some medium-sized company), I had not stopped to think what he might do. Of course, I could never have guessed what his reply would be.

"I'm a companion. Now, don't look so surprised. That isn't what it says on my passport, and I suppose that isn't really my proper title, perhaps private secretary, financial adviser, Manur & Co.'s Iberian representative, whichever you prefer. I was a stockbroker once and that marks you, oh, yes, it leaves a mark, but what can you expect? Basically, though, I'm a companion. At my age there's no point in trying to dress up the truth. And the truth is that I'm just a companion, albeit a well-paid one."

I was still trying to decide if I was interested in this conversation or not and so I did not reply at once, but in one gulp drank down my glass of milk which was still intact before me, and which gave rise to another of Dato's inappropriate remarks:

"I suppose you have to look after your throat and avoid cold drinks. Another whisky, please, barman."

"Yes," I said mechanically. "You must never let your throat get cold, that's absolutely fundamental. For example, I don't usually take my scarf off until well into

June, and even then that very much depends on the weather."

"Really? And when do you put it on again?"

"Usually in early September. If you ever see a young man wearing a scarf around the end of June or the beginning of September, you can be sure that he's a singer. As I say, it's an unforgiving life, with a lot of obligations and duties. We can't even allow ourselves an ordinary cold, which, as you can imagine, would be a complete disaster, because although you might recover soon enough from the cold, it takes four or five weeks before your voice is in perfect condition again. And meanwhile we're in breach or semi-breach of our contract and we lose both money and reputation. But tell me," and I led the conversation back to the one thing that had really struck me: I was struck by the fact that, in the solitude of what had once been my own city, the person now keeping me company claimed to be a professional companion, "What exactly does a companion do? Whom do you accompany? How do you do it? Are you for hire?"

Dato smiled even more broadly than before (he was a nice man or at least that was his intention) and made a negative gesture with one of his delicate hands before picking up his fresh glass of whisky.

"No, you've misunderstood me. I'm not what people call a lady's companion, if that's what you're thinking: you know, one of those insipid, kindly, intransigent women you get in films, looking after some old duffer or an invalid. What I meant to say is that, despite my theoretical duties (as financial adviser, etc.) what I mostly do, my main function and use, is to keep my employers company. Didn't you see them? Didn't you notice? They were traveling with me on the train."

Of course I had seen them and studied them, and analyzed and even defined them: an exploiter and a depressive, a tycoon and a melancholic, a man of ambition and a neurotic. That is how they had seemed to me then, and I had in fact thought about them occasionally since. Yes, I dreamed that at that moment in my conversation with Dato I remembered, or admitted having given them a few fleeting thoughts during the first three days of my stay in Madrid, while I was beginning rehearsals at the Teatro de la Zarzuela for my role as Cassio in Verdi's *Otello*. Given her a few fleeting thoughts. Of course I had seen them, of course I had noticed, but, quite why, I don't really know—or perhaps now I do know—I pretended to think hard for a few seconds.

"Oh, yes, a couple, he seemed very imposing." I hadn't wanted to use the word "imposing," which is so often used when speaking of someone's physical appearance: I had wanted to use an adjective that would describe him morally, but at that moment I couldn't think of any word that would not also prove offensive.

"You've put your finger on it, that's him, imposing. Señor Manur is very imposing. She, on the other hand, is in a terrible state. Not the way she looks, of course, I mean she's very attractive and elegant, but she's a lost soul, really, a most unhappy woman. And she's the one, of course, whom I mainly accompany, both at home in Brussels (he's Belgian, you see, we live in Brussels) and on the occasional trips we make, like on this one now. Especially on the trips. You see, she's got nothing to look forward to and she gets bored. She suffers, she's never happy, and you can see her point really. I'm supposed to distract her, to try to keep her boredom and suffering to a minimum, so that she doesn't cause Señor Manur too many problems, so that she's not quite so unhappy, and focuses on the present and doesn't pine. I listen to her complaints and her confidences, I console her with reasoned arguments, I ask her to be patient for my sake and for Señor Manur's sake too, I try to make her see the pros and the cons; I take her to the movies, to an exhibition, to the theater, to the opera, to a concert; she's very fond of old books and old things in general, and so I consult or, rather, study huge catalogues from the most prestigious booksellers in Paris, London, and New York, and I order for her the most bizarre, most sought-after books, rare, expensive editions, anything that might interest her; and I go to auctions with her, where I do the bidding and raise my finger or make the agreed signal and where we buy not just paintings, but furniture, statuettes, vases, the occasional carpet, wall clocks, letter openers, little boxes, paperweights, engravings, frames, figurines, anything you can imagine, all of it first-rate, all of it very old and in the best possible taste. I do what I can, but, after all this time, I'm running out of ideas and, besides, I'm tired, very tired. I know all her ills, I know them by heart, and she knows by heart all my arguments, my remedies, all my persuasive techniques."

Dato paused to take a sip of his drink. Although he had just begun what appeared to be a litany of complaints, his voice, his gestures, his ingratiating smile had barely altered. It was as if he too were reciting something—a lamentation, the introduction to an aria. And there was not the slightest trace of mockery in his voice, nor even irony. He took that woman utterly seriously and felt no rancour either, perhaps because—or so I thought—she seemed to be his sole occupation in life, even if he would rather she were not.

"The only place in the world where she used to feel comfortable, where she didn't need anything, not even me (*volontiers*), the only place where she had independent memories that predated her disastrous marriage, was Madrid, where she comes from and from where she was uprooted some twelve or fifteen years ago and where, up until only a few months ago, her brother used to live. Whenever we came to Madrid (and since Manur & Co. has traditionally had many dealings here, we used to come here frequently), I could have a rest and devote myself to other things. Señor Manur, as he always is everywhere, would be busy with his many financial deals (he's a banker, you see), and Natalia, his wife (her name's Natalia, you see), would spend all day with her brother. That was the only time when she seemed happy, when she seemed almost to have forgotten her melancholy and seemed almost indifferent to Manur, indeed she was almost nice to Manur when their paths occasionally crossed in the hotel lobby or when they had to go out to some formal supper, to which her brother, Monte, would nearly always go along too. And now what? Monte is no longer in Madrid, he's gone to live in South America (South America of all places!), and for the three days we've been here, Natalia has been even more unhappy and depressed than ever; it's the first time she's been to Madrid without Monte being here, and she's even more bored and lethargic and miserable than she usually is (and for two reasons now), and just at a time when my reserves are at an all-time low, when I simply don't know how to distract her or even how to bring a smile to her face, least of all during those formal suppers. I simply don't know what to say to her any more. I can be quite resourceful when I put my mind to it, you know. I can be extremely resourceful, but she knows all my jokes, all my pithy sayings, the kind of remark I'm likely to come out with, she can even tell when I'm about to make some quip. She knows all my mechanisms and she knows the city, well, she was born here. I can't take her to the Prado or to the Plaza Mayor as if it were a novelty for her. And I haven't got anyone else to fall back on: she's lost contact with all the friends from her youth, because she left here when she was nineteen or twenty, and anyway everyone's always so busy; she hasn't written to or phoned anyone in years and you have to make an effort to keep in touch; all she knows is that in this city, her own city, she doesn't exist: she only used to exist (when she came here) through Monte. She knows the people her brother introduced her to, but they won't want to see her without her brother, you know what social conventions are like and how lacking in curiosity most people are. And I'm finding that here, where I used to have a break, a break from being a companion, I have to work and strain my imagination to the limit; I have to be with her almost all the time, especially during her interminable walks around areas she has probably seen thousands of times before and knows like the back of her hand. It wears me out. I'm too old for all that walking. And besides, Madrid, when it wants to be, is a very hostile city, and here I am obliged to spend hours at a time walking through this hostile city;

walking and stopping again and again (she's always looking at shop windows and buildings), which is the most tiring part of all. What was traditionally my rest period has become the worst time and the worst journey of the year."

Dato finished his second glass of whisky and asked for a single. The suppressed agitation with which he had been speaking seemed to have caused his voluminous, curly hair to fill out or rise. There was still no one else in the hotel bar, just him and me sitting before the invisible presence of the barman. Dato pointed towards the door with one of his small, eighteenth-century hands.

"In a few moments, she'll appear at that door and she won't let me go to bed or continue my conversation with you. No, she'll ask me or, rather, order me to go for a last walk around the block with her, because it's such a fine evening, or she'll want to have a drink with me somewhere so that she can tell me what a terrible time she's had over supper (tonight Señor Manur has taken her to a supper for wives and husbands, part business engagement, part formal supper). And meanwhile he, Señor Manur, will go off to bed so that he can rise refreshed in the morning and dedicate himself busily to his many tasks and occupations. And since I'm no use to him whatsoever (for that's the truth of the matter), he can manage perfectly well without my purely theoretical services; Manur can do everything without my help and I serve a far more useful purpose, a far more valuable role, keeping Natalia company and making sure she doesn't get bored and doesn't suffer and isn't entirely miserable. Do you understand? Do you see? I am a companion, nothing more, and both of them, Natalia and Manur, know that that is what I'm paid to do, and they make that quite clear. And I know it too. So you see, you complain about being too alone; I, on the other hand, complain about having too much company. You complain that your life is too scattered and diverse; I, on the other hand, complain that my life is too concentrated and monotonous. Keeping Natalia Manur company, that is what my life has been these last few years, that is the actual content of my present existence. She's a lovely person, of course, if somewhat on the melancholy side, but only a husband or a lover or possibly a brother can keep a woman company indefinitely and unconditionally, don't you think? And I am not her husband or her lover or her brother. Señor Manur is her husband and Monte is her brother, and she, incredible though it may seem, has no lovers. It's completely illogical in her situation, but that, alas, is how it is."

Dato had spoken these last words with utter conviction, as if—as I think now—he were using them to provoke my incredulity.

"How can you be so sure? Does she really tell you everything?" I asked with due incredulity.

"Well, I don't know if she tells me everything, but, in a way, anything she doesn't tell me doesn't really exist. If it doesn't exist for me, then it doesn't exist for Señor Manur either, and if it doesn't exist for him, then it doesn't exist for me. Do you see what I mean?"

"Not really."

Dato did not seem to have any sense at all that he might be talking too much. In this morning's dream, throughout this repeated conversation, he struck me as a patient and determined man. Determined to tell me, patiently and all in good time, anything I did not know.

"Señor Manur is the one who pays my salary, and, as you can imagine, he expects me to pass on to him any important news regarding his wife. He takes it for granted that if anyone knows what does or does not happen to Natalia Manur, that person is me (since I have been her almost constant companion and probably her only confidant for several years now, he has absolutely no doubt that that person is me). At the same time, Natalia knows what my obligations and loyalties, both theoretical and official, entail, and you will say to me (quite rightly) that she won't tell me anything that she doesn't want Señor Manur to know. Looked at from the other side, though, he assumes that I will know everything about Natalia, at least everything of importance. And since I don't know that she has any lovers (which, generally speaking, is something one would deem to be a fact of some importance), the only possible conclusion one can draw is that she does not. Because the truth is that, suppositions apart, I only know what she tells me. That is all I can know and all I can be expected to know. Now do you see what I mean?"

"Not entirely," I said, although I was beginning to understand the confession of duplicity that Dato was offering me. He seemed slightly impatient with my response, but that impatience lasted only a matter of seconds (his mouth suddenly inexpressive and closed, as I had seen him on the train; his inquisitive eyes bulging even more than usual), but his beaming smile soon returned.

"Are you married?"

"No," I said at once, and although it was true that, in the eyes of the law, I wasn't married, I immediately thought that I had lied and immediately thought about Berta, who, at the time, four years ago, I had been living with for a year. (Yes, although I prefer not to think about it now, it is true that Berta lived with me for some time: and she was always there waiting for me at home when I got back from my operatic travels, which, as I have said, were already quite frequent.) That is, although I didn't lie, I did lie and, as I said earlier, I cannot help wondering if it did not prove to be a decisive lie. Perhaps not. At any rate, it has mattered little during the last few years or, to be precise, now that I'm not dreaming and my dream has ended, it does not matter very much this morning.

"You mean you've never been married?"

"No," I said again, and I suppose I wasn't really lying at all.

Dato took another sip of his drink and looked across at the mirrors at the back of the bar, and reflected in them he doubtless saw Natalia Manur come in, because he immediately turned to me and said in a low, hurried voice: "(Here she is.) Perhaps that is why you don't understand: dealing with a married couple is like dealing with one very contradictory and forgetful person"; and he took a few steps towards the entrance to the bar to greet that woman whom I had seen deep in tormented sleep a few days before. She hesitated on the threshold, half smiling, as if uncertain (as if her uncertainty was not mere politeness, as if, indeed, that was the uncertainty) whether to regret my presence there, which would prevent her from telling Dato about the supper, or to feel pleased at the possibility of meeting a stranger. Her companion accompanied her to where I was sitting at the bar, suddenly very upright, my glass of hot milk long since empty.

WHILE I REHEARSED MY ROLE as Cassio in Verdi's *Otello*, they were both nearly always there before me, sitting—like the other invited guests—in rows ten or twelve in the stalls, so as not to distract us too much by their presence. Whenever there was a pause and I was listening to the director's advice (pure tokenism really, since, in the end, every singer sings the way he or she thinks best and takes not the least bit of notice), I would look at them, especially at Natalia Manur. I asked myself over and over how they could bear these long, repetitive sessions which I myself would have found tedious if they had not been there, if she had not been there. Moreover, the role of Cassio, although an important one, is not a very large part, and very often they were not listening to me (which had been the initial reason for them coming), but to the great but now ageing Gustav Hörbiger playing Otello or to the ghastly, ambitious Volte playing Iago, or to the pair of them in one of their interminable dialogues. If I had to remain on stage, I would just switch off from what was going on there and gaze, fascinated, at those two accidental devotees who had appeared out of the blue in the city of Madrid. Dato, who clearly had absolutely no interest in or even liking for music, seemed, nevertheless, to be permanently absorbed in what was happening on stage, leaning forward, his hands resting on the back of the seat in front and his eyes fixed perhaps on me: as fixed as his eyes had been in the train in protracted contemplation of either the landscape or his own face. Natalia, more relaxed, leaned back (probably with her legs crossed), following our actions with close attention when I was on stage acting and with curiosity—but, I would venture, no more than that—when I was not involved. And when my presence was not required up there, I would come down and join them for however many minutes I had at my disposal. Dato would then almost invariably get up and, so he said, go out to smoke a cigarette, and Natalia Manur, in my opinion—and even though there was no real evidence to substantiate this—would forget all about the illustrious Hörbiger, the grotesque Volte and the lovely Priés (who was playing Desdemona) as completely as I did. I do not know nor did I ever know if Dato took advantage of those moments when I kept Natalia Manur company in order to take a rest from his obsessive duties as companion or if, in his unacknowledged role as Pandarus, he was using that excuse to leave us alone so that we could each gradually become accustomed to the silent breathing of the other or to the way our sleeves occasionally and very lightly touched, so that we could each get used to the faint odour of the other. For the former to be true, he must have smoked three or four cigarettes in succession. However long my break lasted, he never came back until I had rejoined my colleagues on stage: he was probably watching—one swift, bulging eye glancing every few seconds through the crack—hidden behind the curtains that opened onto the auditorium, for Natalia Manur was never left alone for even half a minute: as soon as I resumed my rehearsal, he, with rapid steps and hands behind his back as if still concealing in his fingers the butt of his everlasting cigarette, would return to his seat, and would again, apparently, bestow on me his undivided attention.

Those were extraordinary days. For the first time in my operatic career I did not feel sad and solitary in the big city. On the contrary, in a very short space of time (perhaps only a couple of days) we achieved that wonderfully beneficent state of being in which two or three people take it so much for granted that they will meet up each day that the first question of the morning tends to be "So what shall we do, then?" not "What are you going to do today?" That state, proper to adolescents and to the newly in love, is not without its demands, and one of these, however contradictory it may seem, given one's acceptance of another person or persons as extensions of one's own self and therefore of one's freedom too, consists in the immediate establishment of the strictest possible routine, which leaves no room for any disconcerting improvisations and allows for no catastrophic gaps that might cast doubt on that union and allow room for thinking. Thinking, thinking. Now that

I'm telling you this dream and this story, I realize that I have abstained from thinking for the past four years. The "I" that existed before meeting Dato and the Manurs has been absent or damped down during all that time, and I would go so far as to say that it had died, were it not for the fact that this morning, which is advancing as I write, I seem to recognize that "I." In these pages that I have been filling (without yet having had any breakfast) I recognize a cold, invulnerable voice, the voice of the pessimist, who, just as he sees no reason to live, likewise sees no reason to kill himself or to die, no reason to feel afraid, no reason to wait, no reason to think; and yet he does nothing but those last three things: feeling afraid, waiting, and thinking, endlessly thinking. That was what my mind was like (cold and invulnerable, and perhaps it will go back to being that from now on) before that trip to Madrid. I felt afraid and waited and thought during rehearsals, in hotel rooms, on my walks around cities, in trains and in the few planes I traveled on, in foyers and in bars, as I read scores and studied roles, and (sometimes) during performances, indeed, I remember how, during one performance of *Turandot* in Cleveland, even when I myself was involved and was singing in that unmistakable voice of mine which was already beginning to make a big impression, heralding that final blossoming in Naples that provided me with my sobriquet, I was thinking intently about Berta and me and about how I didn't love her. I used to think so much that I even made my few conversations, especially with Berta but also with other people, a mere verbal extension of my thoughts when I was alone; I used to think so much that I grew bored with myself. It was, moreover, an unreflecting form of thought, unguided, fluctuating, with no goal, no starting point, unbearable; and I had been finding it totally unbearable for some time—and that is not just one more characteristic of the pessimist, it is the main characteristic: being unable to bear that for which there is no remedy or, rather, being unable to bear the only thing that is possible—when I found the salvation and miracle of that unexpected Madrid friendship, which very soon—indeed, at once—was not restricted to the hours I will term "musical": it spread out to fill all the hours of the day, from the leisurely, not too early breakfast taken in the hotel dining room, to the quick or not so quick lunch in some restaurant near the Teatro de la Zarzuela, to the walks, visits, and shopping expeditions around the city, even to several suppers stolen from Señor Manur or, rather—it would be more accurate to say—indifferently yielded up to us. Dato, Natalia Manur and me. We became an inseparable threesome, without the principle of inseparability or the principle of cohesion becoming in any way visible or capable of being put into words, without the profound attraction that Natalia Manur had for me and I for her even aspiring to be so. For the curious thing about those days was that Dato, the apparently indispensable conduit, turned out, in reality—the reality was those breakfasts, lunches, walks, visits, shopping trips and suppers—to be entirely dispensable and neutral: a continuous presence, not just taken for granted but perhaps necessary, yet somehow barely noticeable. With Natalia Manur (or more likely with her and me), Dato was entirely different from the way he had shown himself to be in the hotel bar, as if—again that same suspicion—he were taking advantage of my enthusiasm and my initiative to give his own a rest, or perhaps he remained scrupulously in the background in order to allow me to shine, to let me make myself known. Sometimes, as we were walking along the suffocating, filthy, chattering streets, he would walk a few paces ahead or hang back on the old excuse of tying his shoe lace or looking in a shop window that would be of no interest to Natalia and me (a shop selling buttons, an ironmonger's, not even a tobacconist's or a grocer's), but we usually caught up with him or waited for him to catch up with us, as if not just the fluency of our conversations, but also our very existence there before each other, the possibility of *seeing each other*, depended on or required the impetus of that small figure who had brought us together. When we were sitting at a table, as we so very often were, he tended to keep silent as if he really were just an extra or part of our retinue, and he barely passed any comment at all except on the wine and the food. He also (as befits both a subaltern and a gentleman) dealt with the waiters. He was the one who asked for or chose a table, the one who offered us the menu when we were absorbed in talk, the one who, in the presence of the man taking note, would invite Natalia Manur and me, always in that order, to make our choice of one course, another course, and later on, of dessert and coffee. He showed great insight and good taste when suggesting plans and proposing places to visit, clearly accustomed to having to use his imagination in the accomplishment of his more practical obligations. What he did not do, though, was to pay for what we consumed. I usually did that, although on the few occasions when Natalia Manur insisted, in order, I presume, to show me her gratitude, and when, therefore, I did not pay, I could not help observing that she deposited the money on the small tray along with the bill, and that Dato, having first taken charge of deciding how much tip to leave, blithely picked up any change and put it in his wallet, and Natalia Manur seemed neither surprised nor even to notice. In those two gestures, that of the long, gnarled hand placing notes on the table and that of the tiny, greedy hand removing them, I thought I saw, on those two or three occasions (though possibly more often), the sign of a more important transaction, the emblematic form in which the most secret and unmentionable relationships need, now and then, to be rewarded for their stealth and to be made manifest. Natalia Manur, I thought, was buying or at least maintaining the uncertain nature of Dato's loyalty by paying him considerable sums out of her own pocket; but in that stipulated, periodic payment, the greatest contact between the two of them would possibly be a monthly signature, perhaps not even that. The commercial relationship might be so firmly established—a regular bank transfer made impersonal by habit—that it could almost be forgotten, and those two gestures might well provide a reminder of that link, whereby, for an instant, Dato became the *desired one* and Natalia Manur the *desirer*, she became the determinee and he the determinant. Yes, it was obviously a sign, possibly agreed, possibly demanded by Dato: evidence, momentary but repeated, blatant but deniable, of the true nature of their relationship. That was the only possible interpretation one could place on the permitted pillage of (at most) a few thousand pesetas carried out by that man through the indifferent mediation of a waiter's hand. But it is precisely such actions and such details, sometimes even less perceptible and significant, sometimes in marked contradiction to what they reveal, sometimes deliberate and sometimes involuntary, that allow us to understand, albeit without any proof, the real bias of the relationship between two people, for example, the short, sharp greeting, the fumbled handshake (by hands accustomed to less formal contact), the exchange of excessively opaque glances (painfully censored) between two illicit lovers who happen to coincide at a party accompanied by their respective spouses; or the fearful affability and solicitude (the hand that does not risk bestowing an affectionate squeeze, but instead rests lightly on the other person's arm to usher them past, the ill-timed smile that both regrets and accepts the impossibility of recovering trust or of softening an insult) with which one treats a person whom one has, though without ill intent, nonetheless harmed; like the hands that suddenly clench, the steps that hesitate and then immediately press determinedly forward, when those who either hate or cannot forget one another pass in the street; like Manur's forefinger, which stood erect and still for a few seconds before he gave me his hand on the day that we met, when Dato, always master of the situation, took it upon himself to introduce us: it was a warning forefinger that Manur tried to pass off as a moment's unlikely consideration of my name, which he knew, he said, having seen it in print once or twice ("Once a name has passed before my eyes, I never forget it," he said, "which is not to say, of course, that I can remember to whom that name belongs, only that I can remember having seen it"), he did not know now whether it had been in the review of an opera, on a record or even—which would have meant that he had actually been to see one of my performances—in some theater program ("But, on the other hand, most faces mean nothing to me; and besides, you performers are always so heavily disguised as to be unrecognizable," he said). That forefinger was clearly a threatening gesture, masked only by its fleeting nature; but threats never go unnoticed by those being threatened, especially if when they become aware of the threat they realize (as was my case) that they are in turn threatening the threatener.

The three of us were coming into the hotel as he was going out, but he decided to retrace his steps and even suggested having an aperitif with us in one of the reception rooms ("I have precisely twenty minutes before my luncheon appointment," he said. He had removed his fedora. He looked at his watch). He spoke irritatingly perfect Spanish, with barely a trace of an accent and devoid of any syntactical or grammatical errors (although he did perhaps say "yo" too much). Now and then he stammered over a word, seeking confirmation, but he gave the impression that this was just a childish form of coquetry that merely emphasized the difficulty of the achievement and which is a ploy often used by those who set out to impress. He did not translate from his language or languages ("I'm Flemish and

I learned French as I learned Spanish, only when I was much younger, of course; I'm used to learning," he said. He rejected with a glance one of my cigarettes, and took one of his own). He thought in my language as quickly or more quickly than I. He was pedantic, correct, sententious—possibly unintentionally. He sat down on a sofa, beside his wife, and I remained—stiff and uncertain, hoping that he would be with us for precisely twenty minutes and no more—in an armchair next to him. While he addressed himself mainly to me in my condition as novelty (as one does with foreigners, although he was, in fact, the foreigner), he stroked Natalia Manur's left hand with his right hand. Sitting together like that (how was it possible that I hadn't realized this in the train, I thought during those precisely twenty minutes, and I kept thinking this morning in my dream) it was patently obvious that they were married and had been for a long time. Manur, the Belgian banker, was one of those people, and there are many like him among those who invite me to sing (that is, among impresarios), who mitigate their intrinsic coldness with a perfect knowledge of the formal details that can transform a proud, unfeeling individual into someone attentive and seductive. It was not just that it occurred to him to order the slightly exotic drink for which everyone else immediately opted too (it was, I think, Natalia Manur who blurted out: "Oh, what a good idea") nor that his movements revealed not only the absorbing activity from which he had just emerged and which still awaited him, but also the spirit of insouciance that he had resolved to allot to that precise period of twenty minutes, nor that his smile, calculated to the millimetre, varied depending on whether he was raising his glass to Dato (just enough of a smile to be polite and magnanimous, just enough to underscore his position), to Natalia Manur (just enough of a smile to be ardent and masterful, just enough to underscore her position) or to me (just enough of a smile to be admiring, distrustful and paternal, just enough to underscore my position as clown). It was above all his skill in giving importance to everything that was mentioned in his presence and that was going on around him ("What a useless waiter, doesn't he know that one should pick up a glass by the stem not the bowl," he said; "That's a very bold tie you're wearing, Dato, tell me where you bought it," he said. He speared a pitted olive and ate it. "You might not think so now, but it's time they had these sofas reupholstered: you'll see, in a couple of months' time they'll be starting to look worn," he said. "The human voice is the most extraordinary and complex of musical instruments, in which, contrary to what most people think, the actual quality of the instrument is far less important than the intelligence—the musical intelligence, I mean—of the person using it," he said.

He cast a furtive glance at the nails on one hand), all of which revealed how very difficult it was for him to give real importance to anything. Or perhaps only to Natalia Manur, I thought, for during the precisely twenty minutes he afforded us, he made not the slightest reference to her nor to how she was dressed nor to the delicate glow in her cheeks that day nor to her expression which had grown even more melancholy than usual the moment she spotted Manur in the lobby. He limited himself (but to define it as a limitation might be an attempt at attenuation or a mere inexactitude) to looking at her occasionally with unsettling devotion and to stroking her hand gently but doggedly, a gesture whose very lack of ostentation only made it appear all the more possessive; and she, who formed part of that rambling conversation and who had undergone only the change I have just referred to when she came through the door and saw, advancing towards her, his robust figure crowned by that unequivocally un-Spanish fedora, allowed herself to be touched by that Belgian banker with his rough features and studied manners (a tycoon, a man of ambition, a politician, an exploiter) for precisely twenty minutes. For five or six days, Natalia Manur—despite the married name she had when I met her and with which I will always identify her—had been *my* companion, and in turn brought along her own innocuous companion, the diligent, indispensable, perfumed Dato. And now, suddenly, despite there having been no misunderstanding between us, despite the fact that the implied promise or idea we had been in the process of becoming had not been denied or suffered a sudden deterioration or been overshadowed by some breach of faith, despite our not having changed city or hotel, there I was, watching her allowing herself to be touched by a charming, bald, moustachioed authoritarian, who, like her, was called Manur. Up until then, Manur's existence had been only a fact, assimilated and filed away; or, if you like, had also been a face, interpreted and forgotten. I remember that when we said goodbye, and all four of us got to our feet, Manur kissed his wife on the corner of her mouth, shot his secretary a sideways glance, and shook my hand for the second time, with a distinct lack of cordiality. Then he raised that threatening forefinger again and repeated my name, to indicate that from now on he would know exactly who I was ("I'll think of you the next time I go to the opera," he said. "Although that might not be for a few years: the truth is that I have very little time to myself." He put on his fedora. He looked at his watch.)

That was the second of only three occasions on which I saw Manur, although, shortly after that, I took his place, and since then I have not ceased to see him in my dreams, as always happens in cases of supplantation. It was that raised, rather plump forefinger that made me realize that what I wanted above all else was to destroy that man and to continue seeing Natalia Manur every day: not just in Madrid, not just with Dato, not just while I was rehearsing Verdi's *Otello* in the Teatro de la Zarzuela in what had once been my own city.

I HAVE NOT THOUGHT FOR FOUR years. By this I mean that I have not thought about myself, the only mental activity to which I previously used to devote myself. I used to think about myself preferably at night, before I turned over, once I was in bed, turning my back on Berta or on no one, depending on whether I was at home or staying in some luxury hotel room. When I was at home, the last thing I would see just before falling asleep was a wall because Berta preferred to sleep facing the window and, although I would have preferred that too, I always gave in on those occasions when there was only one of something. My character had largely consisted of giving in, and it still does now. I have only been able to reject things or to fight for them with my thoughts and, lately, as I say, I do not even think. Perhaps that is why I would be best off on my own, so that there is no possibility of my rejecting anyone or fighting with anyone. Nevertheless, there has almost always been someone near, and one of my last thoughts before closing my eyes used to be that no one, not even Berta who was lying beside me, would *really* be watching over my sleep, and that during that prolonged state of unguardedness and oblivion, I would be lost if anything bad were to happen to me. Not that Berta neglected me (she would say goodnight and give me a kiss), but she was incapable of understanding my sleep or of understanding me in my sleep. It is terrifying how people are simply abandoned with an absolutely easy conscience on the part of others, as if it were perfectly natural, to long, hazardous hours in which it is taken for granted that they do not need anything *because* they are sleeping, as if sleeping were in effect what so many literati have liked to say it was: a suspension of all vital needs, the closest analogy with death. People sometimes struggle to understand each other, not that anyone is really equipped to understand, that is, to see the totality of what exists or does not exist. But at least they pretend to be struggling to do so during the day. On the other hand, no one bothers or makes the slightest effort to understand our sleep, for although, in Spanish, the word for "sleep," "sueño," also means "dream," our sleep is not the same as our dreams, which have already been subjected to far too many explanations. Berta, at any rate, had not even paused to consider the idea that our mind and our body continue the same in the nocturnal realm, indeed for her—as I saw quite clearly from the first night we spent together—my whole person ended or was interrupted, ceased to exist, was cancelled out, the moment we fell asleep, especially the moment when she fell asleep; whereas I, conscious that Berta required as much attention and care asleep as awake, would lie for a long time with my eyes open, vaguely thinking about myself and staring at that wall decorated only by an enormous Italian calendar (*febbraio, maggio, luglio*), in order to accommodate as best I could her sleeping mind and body, and trying to accustom myself to the idea that my own sleeping thoughts should understand *her* sleep, that is, understand her as she slept. Sometimes, for that reason, I would lie awake for two or three hours, watching over Berta. The bedroom in our apartment in Barcelona in which I thought and watched and slept was rather on the small side, because, as I have heard so many other couples say, it's a shame to waste space in an apartment on the bedrooms, when they only need to be big enough to take a bed. I wasn't then as famous as I am now beginning to be, I didn't earn much money, the apartment was small too, at least in comparison with where I live now. Now my bedroom isn't small, nor am I faced, as I go to sleep, by a wall, because there are windows on three of the four walls. It is full of light and there is more than enough space. I sleep in a larger bed, in a vast bed with lion's feet carved in wood. Now I am the Lion of Naples, León de Nápoles, however ridiculous it is for me to say so, especially when I no longer know whether the sobriquet flatters or offends. And while I have been transformed into the famous León de Nápoles, Berta is dead and has been transformed into nothing. About three weeks ago, I heard from a man whom I do not know and who, as he explained in his letter (written in a neat, troubling, sloping hand), had married her and lived with her (that is, he had done almost the same as I had done for one year, five years before) for eighteen months, which turned out to be the last eighteen months of Berta's life. He assumed that I would want to know that this person no longer existed. Indeed, he gave me only facts (he refrained from describing to me his state of mind, his despair or his relief), for which I was grateful, for in that way, Berta's death—just facts, detailed but dispassionate—seems to me rather like those deaths shown on television or reported in the newspapers, and so, although it is true, I can allow myself not to understand it. They lived, he told me, that man whom I do not know and whose name I cannot even remember now (but it began with an N, Noriega or Navarro or Noguer), in one of those houses in Barcelona known to us as towers, and which are two or three stories high and are found mainly in the upper part of the city. One day ("a day like any other, exactly eleven days ago"), Berta had fallen on the stairs "as she was going down them carrying some books of yours that she still had from the time when you used to live together," and she had fallen so hard and so spectacularly that she had vomited blood "as soon as she stopped falling." A doctor friend or neighbor, evidently incompetent, had failed to establish a link between the two things, instead he had advised them not to worry too much and, after treating Berta for a few minor bruises on her arms and legs, had merely told her to rest for a couple of days, to see how things progressed and to make sure she got over any concussion. Berta did appear to have suffered only minor bruising, apart from the momentary shock of the fall and the sight of her own blood, which shot out of her mouth like a flame and stained three or four steps and which, what with the worry, they had not cleaned up until the following day, by which time it had already dried and darkened, just as my books had not immediately been picked up and indeed had not been put in order "until today." Berta made an immediate recovery and resumed her usual duties, but on the ninth day after the fall, and only two days before that man, Noriega, had sat down to write me the letter, she did not wake up. When her husband awoke ("at half past seven, in order to go to work," although he did not specify what he did), he found her curled up in the bed, with her nightdress all rucked up and her thighs uncovered, facing him and dead, with a smudge of semi-coagulated blood still trickling out—more slowly with each minute that passed—from her pale, half-closed lips. Her husband, Navarro, gave no further explanations, as if the medical causes of her death no longer mattered to him and should not matter to me. Nor did he vent his anger on the negligent doctor or on himself. "I buried her today," he said in the singular, as if he had buried her alone and with his own hands, as if Berta were a pet. "I thought you might want to know." Once one knows the things one knows it is impossible to know whether one wants to know them or not. I don't honestly know if I wanted to know that Berta was dead, but now I do know and that's that, and if I dream about it, it is no longer something imagined or allegorical, merely a repetition of what actually happened. Noguer's letter concluded with those words, although he added a postscript in which he asked me if I wanted to come and collect the books of mine that Berta was carrying when she fell down the stairs; and meticulously, on a separate sheet, he included a list of fifty or so titles, of which I only remembered owning or reading three or four or five: *The Fall of Constantinople*, *Royal Commentaries of the Incas*, *Wagner Nights*, *Our Ancestors*, and *Pnin*. That is how the titles appeared on Noriega's list, with no mention of the authors. He clearly must have heard a lot about me to decide to write when he did not know me at all, which meant that, while I had not thought about Berta (nor indeed about myself) during the last four years, so much so that I did not even want to remember that I had lived with her for a whole year, she, during the last eighteen months of her life and during her only months as a married woman, must have thought about me often enough to have mentioned me to her husband, Navarro, enough for him, on the same day that he buried her, to write to me, giving me all that unsolicited information which I certainly did not deserve, given all those years of total silence and lack of interest on my part. The news, however, must have affected me, otherwise Berta would not have appeared in my dream this morning. And although I have not retained in my memory Noguer's precise name, I can recall fragments of his letter, which I re-read several times two weeks ago, when I received it, trying to imagine what he did not tell me. I cannot help thinking about Berta's furtive death, which occurred without witnesses or warning and in her sleep, something which would never have happened while she lived with me. There is only one thing more solitary than dying without anyone knowing and that is dying without knowing oneself what is happening, without the dying person being aware of his or her own dissolution and end, as may have been Berta's case. There is no doubt, though, that Noriega must have been an inattentive husband, one who did not watch over her sleep with as much constancy and alertness as I did, and in that sense he is as at least as guilty as he tried to make me feel by twice mentioning the books which I carelessly, but with no ill intent, long ago left behind in another apartment in Barcelona, the one that Berta shared with me, the books which—as I understand it—were responsible for her fall. I had never stopped to think about those books, which were destined to occupy a millimeter in the great mound of my forgettings and which, nevertheless, I now learn have been leading, without my knowing or suspecting it, a life of their own "until today," and were the indirect cause of the death of a person whom I know was very close to me and, even more surprising, that they are still *mine*, since Navarro is offering to restore them to me. Why did Berta not get rid of them, rather than take them with her when she moved to begin a new life in the tower where she found her death "on a day like any other"? Why did she not appropriate them and mix them up with hers and those of Noguer, her husband, as married couples do with the remnants of their single lives? Were they—are they—so unequivocally mine? I barely recognize them. And where was she taking them on that very ordinary day? Perhaps down to a smelly, crumbling, rat-infested cellar in order to abandon them there as proof that the hurt I must have caused her was finally over? Or was she perhaps going to dump them out in the steep street, beside the rubbish bins in that unfamiliar neighborhood, so that suddenly, on that day like any other, they would finally be crushed to nothing along with the burst plastic bags full of leftovers, peelings and boxes containing medicines, after years of being kept separate and apart like relics? Or was she, on the contrary, rescuing them from some dusty, gloomy attic on a day which was like any other apart from a feeling of intense and unconfessable nostalgia for the life with me that she had lost four years before? It is Noriega who says that it was a day like any other. Was I present in the unknown life of Berta Viella until the last moment? What would she have been dreaming about when death came to her? And what can Navarro be like, what can he be like, this chosen one who speaks of "commitments" and beside whose sleeping form his chosen one could die spitting blood while still immersed in nightmares and with half her body ("her thighs uncovered") exposed to a bedroom which might have been spacious or cramped, squalid or welcoming, light or dingy, which might have been well-heated or just damp and warm like the whole city of Barcelona? A bad city to die in. I wonder if that bedroom has more than one window and, if it doesn't, would Noguer have been considerate enough to let Berta have the side of the bed that faced it? I should write to Noguer in order to find all this out, but from his letter he did not seem to me a very understanding person nor exactly high class. I would have woken up that night, sensing death with my sleeping thoughts, and then I would have woken her up so that she would not die in such anguish, so that she would not die in her dreams.

But to be honest, it takes an enormous effort on my part to remember Berta, to remember that I lived with her and, like Navarro, slept with her, and that she always did her best to be at home, waiting for me whenever I returned from my operatic travels so that I would not be assailed by the same feeling of misfortune—of arriving in a place where no one knew me and where no one was expecting me—that I experienced in every city I visited as I walked into the hotel room reserved for me. I find it inexpressibly hard to recall her cheerful nature and her diaphanous eyes, the sudden touch of her hands and the ill-matched colors of her clothes, her easy laughter, her child-like smell, her slow way of talking, her impassive back turned to me during my hours of insomnia. The fact of her death adds nothing to her, rather it takes something away: not only is she now nothing in my imagination, in my thoughts, in my life, she is nothing in *her* imagination, *her* thoughts, in *her* life. She does not even have a life. From now on, if such a thing is possible, she will grow in my forgetting.

HOW CAN ONE DESTROY OR supplant a man whom one barely knows, about whom one knows little and with whom one has no dealings? That was the question which, as the last week of my stay in Madrid began, tormented me and came to obsess me, as it did for several minutes (dream minutes, long minutes) in my dream this morning. They were the busiest, most complicated days, during which I had the least free time, the days of our final rehearsals for the première of Verdi's *Otello* at the Teatro de la Zarzuela and the days when everything seemed about to end in disaster: suddenly and belatedly, two days before the first night, ancient, conceited Hörbiger, Otello, announced that he was entirely incompatible with and unable to sing with Volte, who kept deliberately confusing him on stage in order to discredit and outshine him; the slimy, insatiable Volte, Iago, inexplicably showed signs of losing his voice, a claim I rejected from the start as false: an utterly unimaginative act of retaliation, an absolute classic among singers; and the lovely, silly Priés, Desdemona, began to neglect her accent and to fluff her words and then delayed the dress rehearsal for two whole hours, engaged as she was in a tempestuous flirtation with the orchestra's ugly and mediocre first violin (a Spaniard), who was also missing from his post (they arrived within a minute of each other, their hair dishevelled and their lips wet with saliva, she still fastening her costume and revealing her breasts, he with his bow tie in tatters). During that time, the conductor broke several batons and argued with everyone: at one point, when all the principal singers flounced out of the room, all of us with our own reasons for feeling offended, thus leaving him with no opponents, he brutally insulted the peace-loving theater staff, who threatened to go on strike on the days of the performances. Everything seemed to point to either cancellation or disaster. Even I, Cassio, for the first time I can remember, scaled down my sacred daily practice sessions and paid scant attention to my own part, strangely captivated by that of the other tenor—the Heldentenor, the heroic tenor, the *tenore di forza*, Otello, Hörbiger—and distracted by the beginning of my unexpected suffering.

After meeting Manur and seeing his strength, I realized how very brief that extraordinary time was and how it was approaching its end when it had only just started, and that, at its close, I would have to return to Berta's undesired side and to continue losing myself indefinitely in various hotel rooms and to continue shading away into nothing in various other cities and on other journeys with no real point of reference, far from Natalia (whom I would no longer see every day, whom I would perhaps never see again), while the Manurs and Dato would return to Belgium to their ordinary lives of which—I realized—I knew absolutely nothing. I still knew nothing of any substance about Hieronimo Manur, the banker from Flanders, but even more amazing—I realized—was that I knew nothing of substance about Natalia Manur either, about his wife of many years and my companion of seven days. (That may be why I have not yet told you anything about her, about all the things I learned at the time and have found out since.) During our long conversations—with the imperturbable, taciturn Dato as constant witness—we talked about many things, but never about her, that is, never about her history or past or life. I had had occasion to observe her person minutely and with growing (but unthinking) passion: her unhurried gestures (as if, when she moved, space became somehow denser and more resistant), her facial expressions that had grown so un-Spanish (free of anger and indifference), her grave, sorrowful voice that sounded at times as if it were emerging from a cloud of smoke, her prolonged silences, like absences, before she replied to my sudden questions on an endless variety of topics, her liquid, dreaming eyes, the interminable strides taken by her long legs, the look on her face which was perpetually indefinable or dissolving into melancholy, and her occasional laughter too that revealed large, perfect, very white teeth: an African smile. Likewise she had been able to introduce me to her tastes: her taste in food, at the numerous lunches and suppers we had shared and in the occasional patisserie; her taste in clothes, when I went shopping with her a couple of times and watched her touching fabrics with wise fingers and repeatedly appearing from and disappearing into changing rooms, while Dato and I awaited her judgements, only pretending to offer our opinions; her taste as a collector, at an important auction that was held during that period and in which she—via Dato's sharp, ghostly hand, which rose like a stiletto in response to her desires—made off with two paintings (one Díaz de la Peña and a very small Paret), the centenary edition of Flaubert's complete works and a beautiful penknife designed by Ravilious, with a mother-of-pearl blade and a silver handle, which, given its large size, looked like nothing so much as an iridescent dagger. But I knew nothing at all about her history or past or life, apart from the scant information vouchsafed to me in Dato's self-absorbed and fragmentary complaint during the first and only opportunity I had had to talk to him alone (too soon for my curiosity to have learned how to direct its questions) and from the enthusiastic remarks which, rarely and only in passing, she made about her brother, Roberto Monte, that recent émigré to South America. (She seemed to admire him so much that on more than one occasion I wondered if I were not unwittingly merely standing in for him in the city of Madrid; for we had barely spent a minute apart since the day we met, exactly, according to Dato, as she and Monte used to do when they got together; and, like her brother—

I thought—I too had introduced her to a few fleeting people who would not see her again without my being there, although they were not from Madrid and were only the waning Hörbiger, the presumptuous Volte, the irresponsible Priés and the bellicose conductor.) After a week of being unconditionally present, I still had no idea, therefore, about the nature of the ills afflicting Natalia Manur and which Dato claimed to know so well, nor why it was so illogical—according to him— that she should have no lovers, nor the reason for her profound, irremediable discontent, nor why she and Manur led such separate diurnal lives, when to all appearances they did lead some kind of shared nocturnal life, since, each night, when our trio said goodbye in the hotel elevator, each of us going off to our respective luxury room, Natalia and Manur presumably slept together in theirs. Perhaps the Flemish banker's cognac-colored eyes opened the moment he heard the sound of the key in the lock, or even before, when he sensed, as he waited and dozed, his wife's light steps along the carpeted corridor; perhaps Manur, wearing a pair of improbable green silk pajamas (the same color as his incredible transatlantic fedora), would see Natalia leave her jacket and her handbag on an armchair, go to the bathroom and then, back in the bedroom, undress in order to get into the double bed. Perhaps he received her there with warm words and open arms or perhaps he complained bitterly about how late she was or perhaps they did not speak at all and merely lay in the same bed for eight hours from which all diurnal memory was erased, without looking at each other, without touching, not even in dreams, two bodies together night after night, in mutual oblivion, for years. Or it might be that the cognac-colored eyes, slightly paler and brighter than hers, but (by the way) the (exact) same shape as hers, would remain awake (offended, irascible, impatient), pondering balance sheets and transactions and prices or, who knows, speed-reading some novel, possibly with the aid of a pair of glasses imposed on him by age. How would Natalia Manur enter their luxury room? In the dark, her elegant Della Valle or Prada shoes dangling from two of her long, gnarled fingers in order not to disturb the exhausted banker's repose, or, rather, to avoid answering questions? Or perhaps she would make as much noise as possible (kicking off her shoes so that they thumped against the wardrobe door) and put on all the lights to enjoy the vision denied to her all day, that of her absent and beloved and much-missed husband, whose lack she would have tried, palely, to mitigate in the animated company of a burly, talkative and extremely amiable opera singer? "Hello," she would perhaps say. He would already be in bed, wearing those hypothetical glasses, which mask his plebeian features and soften his chilling gaze. "What sort of day did you have? Everything all right? How was work?" Manur lowers his glasses though he does not take them off, and peering over the top of them with eyes accustomed to being flattered by the things of this world, he does not reply immediately. He looks older with his glasses perched on his nose, although he might have pushed them up onto his forehead, like an aviator, and that, on the other hand, makes him look younger. Natalia does not insist, she was probably just asking out of habit. Quite naturally (like someone in their own house, alone or in front of their life-long husband), she goes into the bathroom, turns on the light and starts removing the make-up she had put on for the evening. She uses cotton balls. Manur continues reading his documents or, more likely, takes the opportunity to perfume himself a little (a small bottle of cologne in the drawer of the bedside table) and to smooth the few hairs that fail to ennoble his prematurely bald pate. (A vain man, even with his own wife.) Natalia keeps the door open as she brushes her teeth, then closes it for a few seconds. Manur pricks up his ears, tries to hear the fall of liquid on liquid. Or perhaps, against his wishes, he cannot help but hear it. He has put his documents to one side, thus demonstrating that there was no need for him to look at them, that he had just been killing time until Natalia arrived. Wait. Wait. Natalia reappears, turns out the bathroom light and starts nonchalantly getting undressed, as if there were no one else there (but I don't know if the lights are on or off or if only the table lamp by whose light Manur was reading is still on), because in reality it is almost as if there was no one there: what can it mean to Manur now to see her taking off her shirt, her skirt, even her dark (seamless) stockings? And what can it mean to Natalia that Manur should see her? Natalia Manur is in her underwear now—one or two pieces, I couldn't say—and she glances at the full-length mirror opposite the bed. It is a fleeting glance, lasting only a matter of instants, probably in the half-light. She is no longer young. Her figure would still seem highly attractive and desirable to any man who could see it, and still is to those who do see it, but she notices the changes: a slight generalized slackening; her breasts are not as high as they were when she was twenty (although no one would think to call them "sagging," rather "precisely as they should be"); her flat, firm stomach announces (but only to her) that it will soon cease to be quite so flat and firm; her legs, which once were supernatural, are still perfect—slim and straight—but they are beginning to appear mortal. Perhaps Manur notices these changes too. The sight that Natalia sees today is familiar, changes go unnoticed on a daily basis, then, inexplicably and unfairly, one day, which is in no way different from the previous day or the next, something has altered and that alteration remains. One never knows if the offending defect, the irreversible wrinkle, its progressive deepening, the age spot on the hand, the thickening neck, the vertical line above the lip, the fat, the pallor, a mark, has actually appeared on that precise day or if, on that particular day, one's own sight is simply more penetrating or more courageous or perhaps simply decides quite arbitrarily to notice it. There is nothing new today, no stain that yesterday passed unnoticed, although the scrutiny was only very superficial, a glance, nothing. It is late, Manur is in a bad mood. It's best to keep the preliminaries to sleep short and to try to immerse oneself in it quickly, where we will be safe for at least eight hours, perhaps, with luck, twenty-four. Natalia Manur removes her underwear—probably a teddy—and for a moment she stands naked in the middle of the room, while those piercing, cognac-colored eyes flicker over that clean, unclothed body, seen from the side, in a rather unfavorable pose and in movement. She cannot bear anything but the sheets on her legs at night, so she puts on a pajama top and sleeps with her underpants on, she may not have taken them off (yes, she did; she will have changed them, those worn at night to sleep in are clean, and we can agree now that she wore only one piece of underwear, a teddy, so she must have taken the underpants out of a drawer and put them on). She gets into bed and from there turns out the main light. The lamp on Manur's side is still on. Manur finally speaks: "What did you do today? Did you go out with that singer again? Odd fellow. I don't like the look of him." "He amuses me," says Natalia, "which you never do." "And how far does that amusement go?" asks Manur, his tone of voice unchanged, simultaneously disdainful and neutral. Natalia Manur does not answer, she turns over, like someone wanting to go to sleep immediately, just as Berta used to do when she lived with me, after we had said goodnight. "And how far does that amusement go?" Manur asks again (he has taken off his glasses and now his expression is as incisive as it was when I saw him in the train). "Far enough for me not to want to leave his company until now." Manur does not want to argue, he just wants to know. "Where have you been?" "I want to go to sleep." "Tell me first." "Where we've been every day: at the rehearsal most of the time, the opera opens soon." "What's he like as a singer?" "Very good, I think. Of all of them, he's the one I like best; and now I want to sleep." Manur puts on his glasses again, his gaze moderated: he does not dare or does not want to ask anything else, although in Natalia's answer there are still many hours that remain unexplained, in fact, there is no explanation. But Manur does not care, he knows from Dato what we do or don't do every day, from the morning when we meet in the hotel dining room to the night when we say goodbye in the elevator, that is, from five minutes after his morning farewell to five minutes before this scene takes place. (We, on the other hand, know nothing about his activities in the city of Madrid.) But he will not know what happened today until tomorrow morning when, before the three of us have breakfast together, he and Dato phone each other from their respective rooms, he probably phones Dato, taking advantage of the minutes Natalia spends in the shower. If, however, Manur wants to know if anything new has happened today without waiting until tomorrow, then he has to ask Natalia. Can he wait? He can wait. Perhaps he isn't really interested. Perhaps Natalia doesn't interest him, despite what Dato gave me to understand when he spoke to me of his theoretical obligations and loyalties to his boss. Perhaps Manur feels absolutely nothing when he sees Natalia getting undressed, when he sees her half-naked, when he sees her naked, when he has her warm, smooth, perfumed body next to him for the eight hours that exist in neither of their lives. Natalia is not interested in him either, although perhaps an awareness of his presence makes her feel nostalgic now and then: that awareness comes to her above all from the smell which, for years now (and in better times), continues to emerge immutably from Manur's neck; the unvarying smell that rises up from his chest mingled with the remnants of his usual cologne, which he put on in the morning and perhaps in the evening too, but which he has possibly not renewed now, while she was in the bathroom: no, it is just a trace and it is precisely such traces that give rise to nostalgia. Things that have only just ended and things that do not exist. Thus Natalia Manur misses the desire she once felt from Manur, and she does not yet dare replace it with the desire of this burly, talkative and very amiable tenor. She does not know his smell, or his chest, she has no idea how his large hands would feel if they touched her, or if, indeed, they ever would. The tenor is not asexual, but he does not make his desire for her clear, which is essential if she is to desire him. He is cautious or too respectful, or else he fears Dato and his theoretical loyalties, unaware that Dato is entirely venal, more than that, that he is for sale to the highest bidder, like all those books, penknives, ashtrays, statuettes, carpets and paintings. Or maybe the singer is homosexual, like so many other theater artistes. He might simply be apprehensive—the very negation of love. He never touches her, however lightly, not even in a companionable way as they cross a street or while they are sitting down, elbow to elbow, in the stalls in the Teatro de la Zarzuela during a pause in the rehearsals. León de Nápoles doubtless loathes physical contact. Singers are famous for taking great care of themselves. How would a singer kiss? Would he spray his mouth before or afterwards? Would he, as legend has it, clear his throat with the clear white of an egg? Would his kisses therefore taste of white of egg? And how does egg white taste on its own? What would he do with all those useless yolks? Waste them? Put them all together in a bowl for the moment? Cook them? Give them to some omnivorous pet who would happily devour even raw yolks? Throw them away? Where? And what if the egg is rotten and the singer doesn't realize it and tosses it back and swallows the stinking, clear white of egg that was supposed to clear his throat? Ugh.

But suddenly today it is Manur who touches her. He touches her thigh, naked, supple and firm (although her legs are no longer supernatural). She allows herself to be touched, although only in order to discover how, after all this time, she will receive this invitation or marital advance. Manur touches her with his right hand, which is both new and old, insistent and soft, a touch which is as recognizable as it is forgotten, which comes from a past in all other respects so similar to the present that it cannot even be viewed as the past. Manur slips his other hand beneath Natalia Manur's pajama jacket and strokes her back. Gradually, surreptitiously, like a novice, he makes each caress move gradually closer to the side of Natalia Manur's left breast, until, once it has reached and gone beyond lateral contact, the hand that pretends to be or actually has become inexperienced goes in search of full frontal contact (the hand emerging from the green sleeve). The whole room suddenly smells of him. Natalia Manur does not move, she does not know if she is excited, not even when it is her nipple that receives and acknowledges that touch (by growing hard). She would perhaps prefer not to know about it, she would like to fall asleep instantly and have Manur, her husband, use her as if she were a doll, according to his fancy, with no preamble, to enter her without her explicit consent, without her participation or her waking passivity, without her refusal or her acquiescence, without her knowledge, without her awareness, without her existence, in such a way that the following day they could behave as if that violation of the norm had never taken place. It is too late now for them to be able to talk about themselves the following day. Just as it is too late for them to feel embarrassed about not talking. Their life is such that it no longer allows for improvisation or change, everything was discussed and stipulated a long time ago. The only thing their life allows for is perpetuation or violent cancellation. But Natalia does not put up any opposition to the Flemish banker's resuscitated attempt at foreplay, because it is at once familiar and remote—a remnant, a trace—because it does not frighten her and it is so utterly improbable and because, since she has been in Madrid, no one has touched her at all. She waits. She waits. Manur, however, must want a response; he gets bored, he desists:

he was always an impatient man. His caresses become lethargic and clumsy, even his hand, grown weary, lies dead on her side, abandoning any frontal approach, contenting itself instead with the degree of lateral contact achieved. Having someone's hand resting on your side is rather uncomfortable when you're trying to get to sleep. Natalia Manur slides a bit further over to her side of the bed, the hand moves away, drops limply onto the white sheet like an anaesthetised limb (the hand in the green sleeve). Manur is the owner of Natalia Manur, but today he gives no orders nor issues any demands. He too turns over, as I used to when I saw that sleep had overwhelmed Berta, and I would turn to the wall, bare apart from the Italian calendar (*aprile, giugno, settembre*), and he falls asleep almost immediately. Natalia does not sleep, but she does not want to move for fear of re-establishing contact with her husband's body. If she tries to turn out the light on his side of the bed, she will touch Manur, and he might wake up. And if he wakes up now, when he has only just fallen asleep, he will not get to sleep again. Natalia Manur's left breast aches. Her husband's smell is now dissipating, as if it were a smell he only gave off while awake, as if it were something exuded by his fierce eyes. His eyes are closed now. The lamp on the bedside table will remain on all night and will startle them awake in the early hours of the morning.

NATALIA MANUR TOLD ME NOTHING during those few days, while I, on the other hand, less reserved than she was or with fewer resources for maintaining a dialogue day after day without resorting to the tale of my own biography (with less strength of mind to endure the silences), did tell her about myself—under the disinterested or slightly incredulous gaze of Dato, who, perhaps out of discretion or diplomacy, pretended to be thinking his own inscrutable thoughts whenever I talked about myself—the bare facts of my story or past or life until approximately a year before, that is, up to the moment when I had decided to live in Barcelona with Berta, whose existence I still had not even mentioned. I talked to Natalia Manur (and therefore to Dato) about my sad, solitary childhood; about my then unhealthy plumpness, which had brought me so much mockery and heartache (another view of the world); about my wretched and always abject relationship with my godfather, Señor Casaldáliga, who took me in on the death of my mother—his cousin—and of whom I have always suspected that he might be, as well as my godfather and second cousin, my ashamed and unconfessed father. I talked to Natalia Manur about the painful experience of being a poor relation, with no rights and no aspirations, with not even the possibility of complaining, obliged to live in a state of uncertainty that goes far beyond what might be deemed reasonable, never feeling that one had a home of one's own. I explained to her how, as a child, I was permanently and painfully aware that I could be expelled at any moment from my room—which, purely by extension, I assumed to be also my home—by Señor Casaldáliga, a truly strange and terrifying man: wealthy (I found out afterwards that he was enormously rich), tortured, mean, devious, somber, sarcastic and authoritarian, a judge by profession and the owner of a bank (but this, like so many other things, I only found out when I was older and through third parties: I knew nothing about his activities when we lived under the same roof). I sensed that my being there—as with my schooling, my food and my clothes—depended entirely on his fancy, not on his affection or sense of responsibility or on his clemency, and nevertheless I felt obliged, not so much to gain his respect and to try to please him, as not to gain his disrespect and not be too much of a disappointment. (I haven't seen him for a long time now: four years ago he was still living in Madrid, but it never occurred to me—not once—to go and visit him, although I did send him tickets to the opening night of Verdi's *Otello* at the Teatro de la Zarzuela, to which he did not, as far as I know, come, at least he didn't drop by my dressing room to congratulate me. He's still alive now, having retired to the countryside, where he lives in a vast mansion in the province of Huelva, and we write to each other occasionally, a strange, belated father-son correspondence.) I explained to Natalia Manur how I had to ask permission to do anything: to move from one part of the house to another, from my room to the bathroom, from the dining room to the living room, from the kitchen to the bedroom, to say nothing of going outside and coming back in again. I never had my own keys. He always wanted to know exactly where I was, as if he were afraid I might come across him in a corner committing infamies that no one else should witness. Every move I made required his consent, and if my godfather wasn't at home, then I simply *had to* (this was what he prescribed and what I did not do) wait for his return before I came out of my room: put up with my bursting bladder, put up with my thirst, put up with my hunger; or be farsighted in a way no child, however sensible, unhappy and reliable, could ever be. Anyway, for years I had to avoid the servants (who, distinctly lacking in charity—and not at all enamoured of this fat little boy—promptly informed him whenever I overstepped the mark) and had to be very careful not to leave clues behind of any unauthorized movement: the sponge used to refresh my face had to be left as dry as it was before and in exactly the same position; whenever I gave in to the irresistible temptation to use the telephone in order to discuss the day's homework with my best friend, I had to remember to leave the handset exactly as he had left it, he being left-handed; I often had to walk around in my stockinged feet, like ne'er-do-wells in cartoons or silent films, in order to avoid leaving any telltale muddy stains on the carpet or the floor; any furtive sips of milk—my favorite drink—had to be minimal enough for any change in the level in the bottle to go unnoticed, as would any incursion into the kitchen in his absence; if I listened to the radio—my great passion as a child—I had to return the dial and the volume to the precise position in which they had been before my excited manipulations. I explained to Natalia Manur how, even when I was an adolescent and he could not keep quite such firm control over me, I had to beg Señor Casaldáliga to give me money for really essential things, and how sometimes he would refuse me for days: money to buy soap when mine ran out (mine was cheap Lagarto, not Lux like his) or toothpaste (mine was cheap Licor, not Colgate like his), money to buy replacements for my almost threadbare undershirts or underpants, to go and get my hair cut, to pay for the bus or the tram to and from school. During my childhood and adolescence, Madrid was a hateful place, and the expression on my face was one of permanent abstraction and amazement, like those little children painted by Chardin, elegantly dressed and absorbed in their games—the shuttlecock, the penknife, the spinning top—with the difference that my clothes were tragically ill-made and, although my gaze was as absent as theirs, I had no absorbing toy to hold or to look at. Then one day, I learned how to read a score and began to acquire my own, and singing came to my rescue. But that isn't what I want to talk about now.

Natalia Manur would listen to me as attentively and compassionately as if she were being told of the misfortunes and privations of some Dickensian child, and she told me later, on more than one occasion, that she was, in part, attracted to me because of those stories and because she could relate her adult fate to that of mine as a child. Soon afterwards, I discovered that her history or past or life shared that same nineteenth-century quality. But, as I have said, prior to the performances of Verdi's *Otello* at the Teatro de la Zarzuela, what I mainly came to realize was my own unthinking conviction: I wanted to destroy Manur and I had to destroy Berta in order to go on seeing Natalia Manur without impediment of any kind. We were in odor of cruelty. The second act of destruction was easy enough, since it depended entirely on a decision I had already taken: I knew everything about Berta, far more than was necessary. The destruction of Manur, on the other hand, was far more difficult knowing, as I did, almost nothing about him and nothing at all about his weak points, and having seen his manner and glimpsed his smug self-satisfaction, his confidence in himself and in his qualities, it seemed to

me impossible to make a fool of him in any direct con-
frontation, whether dialectical in nature or otherwise.
He was clearly stronger and more flexible than I was, as
well as more commanding. After thinking it over very
quickly in my room one night (the night before the first
performance, I remember it well), I realized at once
that the only way of putting into effect my improvised
or unexpected plans was to invert the order in which I
have just listed them: I had only to go on seeing Natalia
Manur every day and the destruction of Manur would
come about by itself. As for the destruction of Berta,
which I did not want, I had, nevertheless, to take it for
granted—to put my signature once and for all to a long-
standing sentence—and try to ensure that the whole
process was as brief as possible and did not interfere
with what, from then on, I imagined to be a conquest or
a game. But that same night I found myself plunged
into doubt as to what method to use. Should I speak
openly to Natalia Manur? Declare myself to her in
proper operatic fashion, before there was any kind of
intimate contact between us? Use Dato as mediator? Or
should I try to get her on her own on some propitious
occasion—perhaps in my dressing room—and act like a
classic—that is, old-fashioned—seducer, at the risk of
failing at the first attempt with no possibility of putting
things right later on? The fact that I had formulated to
myself the nature of my feelings ("I must be in love or

under the unknown influence of some powerful fancy to think like this and to feel such desire," I said to myself) suddenly seemed to be a terrible disadvantage that was forcing me to put into action a plan which was more or less premeditated (but which had still not got beyond the meditative stage) and which was forcing me, therefore, to act artificially, instead of letting things continue as they had until then, taking things, not passively exactly, but at least naturally, without forcing or directing anything, in a state of vague, unexpectant waiting. How tiring loving is, I thought. Striving, planning, longing, unable to content oneself with perseverance and immobility. How tiring the real world is, I thought, with its demands to be filled. And how tiring the as-yet-to-be is too. I have had to struggle so hard all my life to fulfill urgent needs: to grow up healthy and sane, to not be the object of other people's mockery, to lose weight, to not give in to my godfather's despotism, to remove myself from his house, to study music, to study singing, to study in Vienna, to leave Madrid, to enter the small, jealous circle of professional singers, to gain respect, to be an international star. So far I have triumphed in everything I have set out to do, and every morning, when I scrutinize myself long and hard in the mirror in order to spot any changes, I feel certain that triumph is written all over my face. I have an agent who looks after me and always tries to get me the best of everything, I travel the world (albeit alone), I make records and my name appears in third or fourth or fifth place on the album covers, I go to luxury hotels like this one (albeit alone), I have enough money and I know that soon I will have much more. I enjoy my profession, I like stepping out onto the stage in costume and transforming myself into many other people, and singing and acting and being applauded for my efforts and reading the ever longer and more glowing reviews in the newspapers of the world's cities. I like the fact that impresarios and journalists from all over the globe call me up to engage me or to interview me in my house in Barcelona. There I live with Berta, whom I may not love, whom I doubtless do not love, as I realized a few months ago during a performance of *Turandot* when Liu's famous pre-funeral arias moved me so much that I was filled by a sense of invincible love whose object was definitely not Berta, although neither was it anyone else, certainly not the singer playing the part of the enamoured, selfless slave (an excellent soprano, but a kind of German barrel, who has the unfortunate habit of spitting all over her fellow performers when she sings and whose name I will not give here because she is still working; indeed, nowadays she is, like me, a rising star). I don't feel excited about Berta; when I get home, I don't feel particularly glad to see her, nor do I feel any immediate need or desire to go to bed with her, I prefer to wait a few days, to watch a lot of television, to calm myself down, to get used to being back again and accustomed to a sedentary rhythm that doesn't really exist, going out to buy the bread or to the newsstand, going to see Barcelona play at home. The fact is that I find it more exciting to have a luxury call girl come up to my luxury room during some of the lonelier nights of my musical travels. But that doesn't make me unhappy, I mean the lack of excitement I feel about Berta. Relationships with other people have not, up until now, occupied an important place in my existence, perhaps because I have been too busy with the progress of my career, with my indispensable daily exercises, with perfecting my art and lavishing care on my voice, with my studies, the constant practicing and, yes, more studying. Now that I am beginning to reap the rewards and having to struggle less, I see that I have found my place in the wheel and that it will just be a question of that wheel continuing to turn as it should—with me on board—for glory and the plum roles (Calaf, Otello) to come my way. I have had a few love affairs, but none of them was very significant and none of them wrought any great changes in me. Berta is actually perfect. Organized, intelligent, discreet, affectionate and cheerful, mad about music, patient with my rehearsals, and most people find her very attractive, although for some time now (more or less since we began living together) I have not found her so (I am more attracted to the prostitutes whom, as I said, I occasionally summon, out of loneliness, curiosity or boredom). She is not odd or melancholy, like Natalia Manur, whom I nevertheless want to go on seeing every day. Why do I want to go on seeing her every day? Perhaps because I want to be like Liu or like Otello, because, at this particular moment in my history or pre-past or life, I need to try to destroy myself or to destroy someone else. Liu is a Chinese slave who is tortured and later kills herself with a dagger in order to save the life of Calaf, whom she loves and whose name the cruel Princess Turandot tries to drag out of her so that she, Turandot, will not have to marry him and can have him executed at dawn, as she has her previous suitors. Liu is a condemned woman, and that is how she sees herself from the start. Whatever option she chooses will bring her unhappiness. Either she dies and her beloved Calaf lives to marry Turandot, or else she confesses his name and lives, but then Calaf will die with the night. In neither case will her love be consummated, so it is a matter of choosing between one happiness (that of the beloved) and no happiness, or perhaps even between two happinesses and no happiness if we accept the idea that dying for the beloved can for the lover be a perfect form of happiness. Perhaps that is why for Liu the decision is clear. Otello's story is even better known. Among his options, he does not even consider anyone else's happiness, unless it were, in an impossible Otello, that of the supposed lovers, Desdemona and Cassio. It is unthinkable, Otello stepping aside to bring about the happiness of his wife and the man with whom, according to Iago, she has been unfaithful. If Otello had lacked, as Liu did, the notion of justice . . . (But the lack of that notion only became acceptable in our century.) Berta is perfect for my career and for my general well-being, but not only do I want to go on seeing Natalia Manur every day, tonight, I thought then, I very much want to go to bed with her, as much as I very much do not want to go to bed with Berta ever again. It was, like nearly every night during that stay in Madrid, a spring night. I had the balcony doors open and I could hear, from outside, the murmur of cars and the occasional abrupt, angry, drunken voice. I could hear noises from inside too, keys opening the doors to other rooms, fragments of foreign conversations in the corridors, a waiter with a tray or with a trolley, knocking on a door; at one point, I heard the climax of a loud argument and something crashing into the wall of the room next to mine, it sounded like an ashtray thrown by a woman at a man, rather than by a man at a woman (he said, in Spanish with a Cuban or possibly a Canary Islands accent: "Well, if you didn't want to know, you know now!" and then she replied: "I'll show you, you bastard!" and then came the bang). Natalia and Manur would never argue like that, it wasn't their style, given their apparent sterility and coldness. Would I become the cause of an argument one day, soon, tomorrow, tonight, already? I tried to stop thinking these thoughts by rehearsing for the penultimate time—or, rather, recalling it, since I sang it to myself in my head—what would be one of my brief interventions the following day in the role of Cassio: *Miracolo vago* . . . *Miracolo vago* . . . and another immediately afterwards, alternating between the two: *Non temo il ver* . . . *non temo il ver* . . . I was murmuring or singing these words to myself over and over, as if, after the third or fourth time, they had stayed in my head against my will, and then everything suddenly happened very fast, just as it did in my dream this morning. The image of Natalia Manur at the supper we had shared, and which had ended only half an hour before, kept going round and round in my head. She was wearing a raw silk dress, slightly décolleté—a spring décolletage—that had made me notice her cleavage for the first time. It is always a serious moment when you notice for the first time one particular part of a woman's body, because the discovery is so dazzling that it stops you looking away even for an instant; it distracts you from the conversation and the other people around, and when you have no option but to turn your gaze towards, for example, a waiter who is asking you something, your eyes, as they return, do not travel through space from one point to another, nor do they slowly take in the view, instead they alight once more, without pause, on the one thing that they want to see and at which they cannot stop staring. It is impossible to behave correctly. Thus I spent the whole supper without addressing a single word to Dato and listening to Natalia without hearing a word she said, responding mechanically and in complimentary tones to her remarks, with my servile eyes almost fixed on the beginning of that space between what seemed to me to be Natalia's extraordinary breasts. It was a banal discovery, but then I am, in many ways, a banal man (sometimes I even do my best to appear vulgar). She must have noticed, and I must have seemed like a complete idiot, if not worse, but, looking on the bright side, any advances I made, now, tonight, would not come as a complete surprise. My desire was very strong that night, as desire always is when it makes its first identifiable or recognizable appearance in one's consciousness. I picked up the phone and asked to be put through to Natalia Manur's room. While I was waiting for the connection—it took, as it usually does, only a matter of seconds—I realized that I was also ringing Manur's room and that it was already half past midnight. As usual, Dato, Natalia, and I had said our goodbyes to each other in the elevator less than half an hour before. She would still be awake and Manur might not yet have returned from his presumed business supper. But if Manur picked up the phone, I would hang up without saying anything, exactly as if I were one of the lovers that Natalia Manur did not have. Manur's voice answered ("Allò?" it said two or three times in French, then corrected itself and said "Hello?" once) and I hung up, and it was for that reason and no other that I had a prostitute come up to my room that night. I realize that telling you this could make a very bad impression and lose me your sympathy, but the prostitute also appeared in this morning's dream, which is, after all, what I am describing to you.

It was not an act of instantaneous despair or of basic spite, nor was it dictated by the impossibility of satisfying my desire for Natalia Manur (I would like to believe that there was nothing in the least compensatory about my decision), rather, I was resorting to a swift, sure way of giving vent to the agitation provoked in me by my hanging up the phone and of filling the sleepless hours that awaited me because I had hung up straight away. The idea of calling a prostitute on the eve of a first night performance was really most unusual, so rarely did I use their services, despite what I said earlier. (And never on special days.) I decided that it would be best to sort the matter out in person, so I went down to the night porter at the reception desk and, very discreetly, although, at the same time, placing some money on the counter, I asked the well-turned-out, respectable-looking fellow who was on duty what chances there were of finding some pleasant company at that hour of the night either on the street or elsewhere. This is a neat way of not involving a reputable hotel in such services by making offensive assumptions, but, equally, giving its employees the opportunity to provide them (I know from experience that even the most venerable hotels, in terms of clientèle and years in the business, can provide such a service, which is, indeed, much sought-after by the potentially suicidal or homicidal traveling salesmen who occasionally stay in them, not to mention businessmen like Manur when they are alone).The night porter looked at me entirely unconspiratorially, recognized me and, with the same care with which he would have explained to a tourist how to get to the Royal Palace, he immediately dissuaded me from going out into the streets ("May I be frank? If you don't know the area and you don't have your own car," he said, pausing slightly to give me the chance to shake my head to both these things, "you could waste a lot of time walking up the Castellana," and, taking out from beneath the counter a map which he kept there already unfolded, he pointed to the Paseo de la Castellana and ran one impeccable finger all along it, "before finding anything worth bothering with, apart from transvestites and drug addicts, because I don't imagine you want anything too central or too popular, do you?" I was struck by his use of the word "popular," which was a polite way, then and now, of referring to the riffraff in the most central part of the city center) and suggested that he might be able to get one of the *staff* masseuses (he emphasised the word "staff" as if that provided some kind of real guarantee, and added "if, of course, you are agreeable") to come up to my room in fifteen or twenty minutes, if I could wait that long. I said, "Yes, I'll wait," and asked him if I should pay for the service separately or if they would add it to my bill, forgetting that the second option was impossible, since it was not I, but the organizers of Verdi's *Otello*, who would be paying. He, more on the ball than I was, opted for the first solution and informed me that the young woman (that was what he called her now—"young woman") would herself furnish me with a bill. Only when he said the word "bill," did he finally pick up the note I had placed on the counter and which had remained there during the whole of our brief conversation, like a mark on the wood—polished, indelible and ancient, and which no one even notices any more. I went back up to my room.

Today, while I am writing this with barely a break (although, driven by hunger, I have just paused at last to have breakfast, thus risking abandoning for ever the nocturnal realm), I very much regret not having behaved in a more relaxed and gentlemanly fashion with the woman who knocked at my door a quarter of an hour later, just as the night porter had told me she would. Perhaps if I had been more attentive and less fussy, things would have turned out differently, with her and with the Manurs. Today (but it's too late now) I offer her my arm when she comes in, I introduce myself, giving my name, surname and profession, I help her off with her coat, I ask her to sit down, I pour her a drink from the so-called minibar in my room, I compliment her on her dress and her smile and the color of her eyes and, when she leaves—perhaps not, as really happened, only ten or fifteen minutes after her arrival, but half an hour or an hour later—I give her two tickets for the first night of Verdi's *Otello* at the Teatro de la Zarzuela and insist that, at the end, she must drop by and see me in my dressing room with her companion, who might well, I think, have been the highly efficient night porter-cum-emissary. In fact, I feel far more curiosity now than I did then about that willing prostitute who had left her sleep or her work (the latter, since she had put off an engagement) to satisfy the whim of a poor anxious, enamoured guest, although, of course, she knew nothing of my enamoured state or of my anxiety.

I remember very clearly that the first thing I noticed when I opened the door was the black coat she was wearing. It seemed odd to me, because people were no longer wearing overcoats at that time of year in Madrid, where, as everyone knows, one passes effortlessly from winter cold to almost summer warmth. Under that overcoat, the prostitute was wearing a minuscule mauve dress which looked as if it were made out of satin, but which might well have been just rayon, and the shortness of the dress may well have explained the coat: you couldn't go walking along the corridors of a venerable hotel in a brief, clinging garment like that. She took it off and put it down on an armchair (the coat, I mean) while I looked her over and asked her straight out, without even offering her a seat:

"What's your name?"

"Claudina. What's yours?"

"Emilio," I lied, absurdly, since the night porter not only knew my name and doubtless my status, he also had all my details at his disposal, including my Barcelona address: if he wanted, he could even blackmail me on my return home. And what would Berta say if she found out? Then I remembered that Berta was no longer going to be part of my life.

I looked more closely at the face emerging from the mauve. This prostitute was rather attractive at first glance, with large, sinuous features and a suitably dissolute, somewhat salacious look on her face. To judge by the little attention she was paying me (she was not looking at anything in particular, and certainly not at me), she did not, however, seem overly enthusiastic; I mean that she did not seem prepared to pretend an enthusiasm for her job which some clients expect and for which they are extremely grateful. She was the type, I thought, who thinks it enough simply to be. I closed the balcony doors and then the silence grew still longer.

"Where are you from?" was the next thing it occurred to me to say, or the next thing I wanted to know. This is the kind of question one can only ask in capital cities.

"I'm from Argentina. What about you?" asked Claudina the prostitute without the slightest trace of an Argentinian accent.

But I was the one who was going to pay and I wanted to direct the conversation, and although I was in the mood to ask questions, I certainly wasn't in the mood to answer them.

"Ah, I see. From Buenos Aires?"

"No, I was born in the pampas, in the province of Córdoba."

This statement, just in case there was any doubt, was made in an unequivocally "popular" Madrid accent, which is why it began to seem pointless to continue a conversation in which the person being questioned was not only systematically lying (which was perfectly normal), but was not even making the slightest attempt to lend verisimilitude to the deception. Nevertheless, I wanted to see how this undeniably Spanish prostitute with her modest fantasies would cope. She had an acceptable figure, and her face—as I was able to confirm on somewhat closer inspection—was quite attractive, although, as is often the case with women in that profession, it was spoiled by the exaggerated mouth movements she made each time she spoke.

"And what does the Córdoba over there think of our Córdoba over here?" It was an idiotic question, of course, but precisely because of that a particularly difficult question for a Madrid girl who had probably never been out of the country and, therefore, an excellent question with which to test her imaginative powers. It bothered me that she did not want to answer it: hiring a prostitute also means, in large measure, acquiring the right to dictate a performance, and her reaction annoyed me in exactly the same way as, when I was child, it used to annoy me if, during our games of make-believe, my playmate did not stick to the plot and to the dialogues that I had thought up for each occasion.

"Look, Emilio," she said, "I haven't got much time, you know. I'm already running late for another appointment I made earlier. Don't get me wrong, but I only made time for you because Céspedes asked me to."

So Claudina the prostitute called the night porter-cum-emissary "Céspedes," I thought, and I immediately wondered what Natalia Manur would call me, by my first name or by my surname, when she mentioned me to Dato or to Manur himself. The hum of cars became audible again, once our ears (mine) had grown accustomed to that longer silence. However, all my agitation and my vitality were draining away after only a few minutes' exposure to the indifference and conversational ineptitude of this other person. My discourteous attitude had been a mistake, but, after all, I thought, it is usually women who set the tone in any encounter or conversation. Even Claudina the prostitute was capable of disarming me and dissuading me from my initial intentions simply by not looking at me. I was glad that I had not forced a second encounter with Natalia Manur that night: if she too had failed to look at me, I might very well have ceased to desire her, just as I no longer felt the slightest desire for Claudina the prostitute after only five minutes of her indifferent, lying, unimaginative, weary, and (my fault this) still standing presence. Nevertheless, I tried to make my position clear.

"Well, in that case, at least allow me to decide how I fill the time," I said sourly.

"All right, I've got twenty minutes." And she looked at her watch just as Manur had looked at his on the one occasion when I had spoken to him. "What do you want me to tell you about? Not my childhood, please."

No, that wasn't the way. Now I really did feel offended, and the fact is that I did not want her to tell me anything, just to entertain me in my own way, to change personalities for a while, to act, perhaps to play. I should not have treated her like that, she had taken offence and had proceeded to treat me coldly and precipitately. Any possibility of a novel conversation or drama and the harmonious and fair distribution of roles had been spoiled from the start.

She had sat down at last when she said "all right" and now—legs crossed, her gaze still distracted, wandering here and there—she was revealing the whole of her thighs, so I sat down in turn on the left arm of the chair and touched them lightly—full frontally—with my fingertips. She immediately uncrossed her legs to make it easier for me to do so, but there was nothing provocative about this movement, it was made out of sheer indolence. Her thighs were softer than they looked, in fact, they were too soft and had a scar-like texture that did not make them exactly pleasant to the touch. At that same moment, I noticed that Claudina the prostitute was not dark-skinned enough to wear the color mauve. She should have waited a little longer, until the summer, to wear that dress, but she probably didn't realize that. Prostitutes are not educated in colors. I continued touching her, with my whole hand this time, and her pale, soft thighs, firm and smooth, artificially taut, suddenly reminded me of my own thighs when I was a boy (a fat boy) and when I had no option but to see them all the time, because my godfather did not allow me to wear long trousers until I was sixteen years old, on the pretext that the continual rubbing of my plump legs would wear the trousers out. And although Claudina the prostitute's thighs were slim and shapely, I had the feeling that I was touching the thighs of a former me. I found the thought troubling. Claudina the prostitute opened her legs slightly, offering me her inner thigh, but she did so lethargically and hastily, if those two qualities can coexist.

"No," I said, and she, slightly bemused, finally fixed her grey eyes on me. I closed her thighs and got to my feet. I picked up her unseasonable overcoat from the other armchair: it was a gesture that brooked no appeal. "It would be best if we just take this time as filled and you get off to your next appointment. Have you got the bill? The night porter said you would bring one."

"There's no need to be like that, I can always be late for an appointment," said the prostitute, still seated, with a touch of amour propre and a tone that bordered on the conciliatory, just the bare minimum of conciliatoriness to allow money to change hands, however well or ill gotten that money might be, however it was obtained.

But there was no point in starting all over again. I had absolutely no wish to remain with Claudina, especially if I couldn't have a quiet conversation with her and ask her, for example, how it was that she had such a strong Madrid accent, if she had been born in Argentina.

"You haven't even got an Argentinian accent," I said as I handed her three or four (I can't quite remember) of the same notes I had handed to the night porter for the favor.

"What do you mean?" she replied with genuine surprise. "I've done everything I can to get rid of my accent, but I just can't do it. I should know, I've lost several roles in the theater and on TV because of it."

I did not sleep well that night. I had murky dreams that this morning's dream chose not to reproduce. But at least I managed to get to sleep as soon as I was alone, tormented in the midst of the ever longer silence of the city by the belated doubt which I will now never be able to resolve, whether Claudina the prostitute was, after all, a real Argentinian and a magnificent actress, who had managed miraculously and unwittingly to suppress all trace of her origins, or if, on the contrary, she was an extremely stupid girl from Madrid doing her level best to disguise her accent and thus give some verisimilitude to her lies, although, if that were the case, only she would ever know. When I closed my eyes, after looking briefly at the empty wall and thinking, as I used to then, that this would be yet another night spent with no one watching over my sleep, the whole room still smelled of

Claudina the prostitute, and the truth is, it smelled good.

INSTEAD OF BEING HERE WITH THIS pen and these sheets of paper for the better part of the day, I should have been studying the new role, in yet another Verdi opera, that I will soon be singing in Verona and in Vienna: it will be the first time I will have sung the role of Radames in *Aida*. A tenor has no option but to sing Verdi all his life unless he specializes in Wagner, something which I haven't done and never will do. Wagnerian singers are obsessive creatures and tremendously finicky, or, rather, as well as being finicky—as we musicians all tend to be—they insist on trying to appear original both in their singing and in their habits, and that desire, as everyone who has had any direct contact with the production or transmission of the art will know, is the most maddening thing there is. I myself have many eccentricities. (For example, the pen I am writing with at the moment has, as do all my other pens, a matte black nib, because a shiny, gold nib—as most nibs are— would hurt my eyes which, as I write, inevitably remain fixed only millimetres away from that gleaming nib as it scratches over the surface of the paper.) But I will never reach the same extremes as Hörbiger, who, although he had already appeared in Madrid four seasons before in the role of Otello, sang mainly Wagner, especially the

Wagnerian roles of Tristan and Tannhäuser. In his day, he was a brilliant and innovative interpreter of these roles, but his craving for originality grew gradually stronger and more all-encompassing as, over the years, his powers declined, and in the latter part of his career, he used to boast about his own eccentricities and say very proudly that in order to feel even moderately well, he needed to have eleven hours' sleep a night, to change his clothes four times a day, to bathe three times and to make love twice. If that were true, I really don't know how he had time for anything else. But his real mania and his real obsession was that he could not set foot on the stage if, from his hiding place behind the curtain a few moments before the performance began—one swift, bloodshot eye coinciding every few seconds with the crack in the curtain—he could see that there was a single stalls seat empty. He didn't care what was happening in the circle (although he preferred it to be full), but, accustomed as he was to the constant ovations of his youth, he could not abide there to be any gaps in the stalls or in the boxes. However, this is precisely the situation a minute before any performance begins, because there are always some members of the audience who come late, and Hörbiger would make the impresarios raise the curtain five, seven, ten, twelve, even fifteen minutes later than the appointed hour in order to allow time for the stragglers to arrive, so that he could peer out and find that all the seats in the stalls and the boxes were occupied. Those who had arrived promptly would grow irritated and, to the anguish of their ears, the orchestra, grown bored, would keep tuning and re-tuning their instruments. But despite these generous delays—to which the organizers of these events always agreed beforehand in order to avoid Hörbiger's bouts of despair, his loud yells (sometimes audible on the other side of the curtain), his threatened fainting fits and his insulting remarks, for he was always quick to brand the organizers as incompetents or saboteurs and to accuse them of having plotted with some vengeful colleague by not advertising his performance widely enough—there are always season-ticket holders or invited guests who fall ill or are away traveling and forget to hand on their tickets to friends, and so Hörbiger, once he had grasped this problem, was in the habit of tirelessly and boorishly nagging the other singers and the conductor to make sure, when using their quota of invitations, to give them to people who would, under no circumstances, fail to turn up or else would take care that someone went in their place. And not content with this, he would demand that the impresarios should have at least fifteen or so employees or hired hands ready in the theater corridors ("They do it on television, don't they?" I heard him say in loud, threatening tones to the mayor of Madrid himself—the late mayor), who, if there was a problem, and if, after a quarter of an hour's postponement, there were still empty seats, would irrupt into the auditorium and, without delay, eliminate any lacunae. Hörbiger's problem grew more acute with every season, and from having been a real genius in his youth and an artist of immeasurable talent in his maturity, during his latter years, he rapidly lost both voice and artistry, and attracted fewer and fewer people to each performance he gave, so that gradually the admission time for stragglers was extended further and further (but they, for their part, fully aware of Hörbiger's obsession and reluctant to endure the inevitable waiting, arrived later and later, thus closing the vicious circle) and the number of employees or hired hands, who had to be ready when the order came to intervene and occupy those irremediably empty seats, grew larger and larger. At his last appearances, colleagues say that the corridors and the foyers of the respective theaters in which these took place were peopled by strange, tie-wearing rustics whom one could tell had never been to an opera before in their lives and who—being doubtless exclusively television viewers—did not even seem to know that they should keep quiet during the performance. And on his very last appearance, in Munich and again in the role of Otello which I saw him play, they say that more than half the stalls seats were filled not only by these false aficionados or hired laborers and by the very few spectators up in the circle who had been invited to come downstairs—to the fury of those who had paid more for their tickets—but also by all the ushers, porters, cloakroom attendants, cleaning women and even box office staff, whose presence was so urgently needed that they did not even have time to replace their uniforms, overalls and work clothes for something more presentable, even if it was one of those twisted, clumsily-knotted ties which, only a short time before, had sufficed to fill other theaters and which Hörbiger had never imagined that all too soon he would miss. That day, in Munich, not far from the summer scene of his greatest Wagnerian triumphs, the mighty Hörbiger brought his incredible career to a close in a way that was as fitting as it was unexpected: when, forty-five minutes after the hour appointed for Verdi's *Otello* to begin, and when, as I have said, they had recruited everyone in the building (they even had to resort to vital behind-the-scenes workers) to fill up the stalls and the boxes; when, as I say, the most admirable Heldentenor or heroic tenor of our times once more pressed his reddened eye to the opening in the curtain and, with the help of a small Japanese telescope which he sometimes used to inspect the vaster auditoria, he espied with horror an empty seat in the antepenultimate row of the right-hand aisle, an extraordinarily shrill note that no one has ever been able to repeat, and for which the word "moan"—they say—is but a poor definition, echoed round the whole theater. I suppose that last, irredeemably empty seat finally upset the balance of his already fragile sanity, for the fact is that, in full Otello costume, with his blacked-up face, his wild, curly wig, his eyes and lips made to look bigger with makeup, an earring in one ear and his telescope in his hand, the magnificent Hörbiger stepped onto the stage, climbed down into the stalls area, strode through it, to the astonishment of an already irritable public, and sat down in that one accusing seat, thus completing the audience that had been his downfall. When the conductor in person (Parenzan, an old friend of his) went to fetch him and, with kind words and great tact, tried to persuade him to return to the stage in order to begin the performance, assuring him that he would go straight out into the street and invite some passer-by to occupy his seat, Hörbiger, completely deranged by then and unable even to recognize Parenzan, the colleague who had shared in so many of his triumphs, started yelling that he had paid to see and hear the "divino" and that he had no intention of leaving his seat or of giving up to some interloper a ticket for which he had been forced to scrimp and save for months and then to stand in line for days outside the box office of that ghastly theater. And it was high time, he shrieked indignantly, that they stopped messing about and began the perform-ance. The audience picked up on that one phrase and applauded it, thus unconsciously recognizing the tenor's double role and unwittingly giving a last ovation to the cause of his malaise. Hörbiger left the Munich opera house dressed as the Moor of Venice, borne thence by his colleagues Iago, Cassio, Roderigo and Montano, who had no option but to drag him forcibly from that far-flung aisle seat, amidst a genuinely mutinous audience. Hörbiger has not performed since. I don't know where he is now, and I prefer not to think about it as I fix my gaze on the black nib scratching across the paper, because I fear that it may be a place where they encourage him to sleep out his indispensable eleven hours and allow him to bathe and to change his clothes as often as he likes, but where it may prove difficult for him to enjoy his twice-daily love-making. Whatever the truth of the matter, what one can say to his credit is that, however fantastic and fraudulent his methods, the great Hörbiger always managed to fill the stalls and the boxes in every theater from the night of his debut to that of his unexpected retirement, although in order to achieve this, on that last night when he uttered only one note and heard only one ovation, he was obliged to transform himself into the most impatient, unstinting and long-suffering spectator of himself. Poor, great Hörbiger. A similar end, or one not much better, awaits us all, but I am convinced that the reason Wagnerians are the most prone to such spectacular collapses is their excessive love of originality. That is why I am not a Wagnerian and never will be.

All this happened two years ago. Four years ago, the situation was nowhere near as serious, but even then Hörbiger made a point of sharing the billing with other acclaimed or up-and-coming singers who would themselves pull in the audiences, for he was aware, within his progressive limitations, that he was no longer enough to fill auditoria. The acclaimed singers in Madrid were Volte or Iago and Desdemona or la Priés; I was the promising younger artist. Something promised provokes unease and thus is more attractive than something already given or confirmed, and that is why it was no great surprise that on the day of the première of Verdi's *Otello* in the Teatro de la Zarzuela, of the four main singers, I was the one most sought after by the journalists, although I don't deny that my nationality (which I have still not renounced) had something to do with that and the fact that none of my fellow stars spoke any Spanish. Be that as it may (and I remark upon it only in order to make an observation before I go on), from the moment I woke promptly the next morning, with a hint of cheap, pleasant perfume still lingering either in my memory or in the room, the telephone did not stop ringing. So much so that when it rang for the fourth time, as early as half past nine, while I was shaving before going down to have breakfast in the inevitable company of Dato and Natalia Manur, I was tempted not to pick it up and to ask the exchange not to put any more calls through. But (and this is the observation) in the whole of that dream and in the whole of the prelude to my love story with Natalia Manur (of which the dream almost entirely consisted) there has been and there was a mixture of the intentional and the involuntary, as if all intention needed to do was to peep out, to announce itself, to arise in embryonic form or to put in the briefest of appearances, in order for its barely glimpsed or hinted-at plans or desires to find themselves presented with the very circumstances that would make them possible (or would make possible the persistence of that imminent intention) and which owed nothing to my still only incipient and never-confirmed desire to carry them out. I believe that in those moments, as in so many others in this prelude, there were no real attempts, tricks or efforts or even actions on my part, although I don't know if that exempts me from all responsibility for what happened next and for what is happening now. But something intervened, something which, nevertheless and consequently, could not be called fate or even so-called chance. A hand perhaps. (A tiny hand, an index finger perhaps.) I can only explain it by approximation, as is, moreover, my natural tendency: it was as if I did not have to do anything, I merely had to think of doing it, which is more or less what happens to us when we dream. That is perhaps why this history or past or fragment of life seems more believable now that it has ceased to be only reality and, from today, is now also a dream. Because nothing and no one questions dreams, there's no arguing with them nor do they require justification. Dreams simply tell themselves, in the order in which they happened and with their definitive images, and anything can happen in them, even the non-existence of Natalia Manur: for this morning I did not see her clearly once, she was not a real presence and barely had a voice, and that is how I am describing her to you now, you who cannot see her face, can barely hear her words, just as I myself could not see her face or hear her words, despite the fact that I know both face and words so well. It is possible that this morning she was only a name, Natalia Manur.

I DROPPED THE MIRROR ON THE bed and, still holding my electric shaver in my other hand, I picked up the phone; and I recognized the voice at once, the same voice that had so easily scared me off the previous night. There was no mistaking his voice, despite his lack of any foreign accent in my language: assured, resonant and rather deep, although more of a true baritone than a bass baritone, if I say more Jokanaan than Wotan, some of you will know what I mean. I did not have time to beat another retreat: I could have hung up after the irritable "Yes?" with which I greeted this further interruption (Spanish telephones work so badly) and then simply not have answered any second attempt on his part to get through; I could, meanwhile, have sought out Dato or Natalia Manur herself, I could have found out what was going on, prepared myself, allowed myself to be guided by them. But I did not think quickly enough and said "Yes" again, this time affirmatively, in response to that emphatic voice that had appended a question mark to my name.

"It's Hieronimo Manur"—that is how he said his own name, at least in Spanish, with an aspirated "h" but with less stress on the second syllable than there would have been in any Spanish *Jerónimo*—"Natalia's husband, we met a few days ago, as you will remember. I know that tonight is the first night of your performance and that you must be very busy"—he spoke quickly, admitting of no interpolations, like someone despatching what you might call the formal business at the beginning of a meeting—"but I would like to speak to you as soon as possible. Would you mind if I came to see you in your room in about five minutes?"

In fact I minded very much, a visit from Manur just before a first night or indeed at any other time was definitely not in my plans, but his resolute, naturally authoritarian tones, prevented me from saying so outright.

"Well, actually, I was just getting shaved before going down to breakfast with your wife and Dato, your secretary. Why don't we meet up with them in the dining room? What is it about exactly?" I made the stupid mistake of asking two questions at once because, in such cases, one question, usually the most important one, always remains unanswered.

And Manur (as I think I knew from the very first moment) was an intransigent (a tycoon, a man of ambition, a politician, an exploiter).

"No, I'd rather talk to you alone. If you want to finish shaving, I'll order two breakfasts to be brought to your room for us. What would you like, tea or coffee?"

"Coffee," I replied as automatically as I have always replied to that unvarying question in endless luxury hotels; and with that reply, I suppose, I agreed to receive Manur, for all he said was: "Fine, me too. See you soon then," and he hung up.

Manur did not give me the five minutes he had not so much announced to me as imposed, instead he gave me the ten minutes I so much hoped for.

I wasted at least the first of these minutes listening to the phone ringing vainly in Dato's room. I did not dare to ask for Natalia's room again, because Manur himself would still be there—always assuming that he was giving me the extra time I so craved. After some hesitation, I asked to be put through to the dining room, in the hope that my habitual companions would have already arrived. The person who answered took no fewer than three minutes between putting down the phone and locating Dato, at least that is the amount of time that passed before I heard Dato's voice at the other end.

"Hello," he said. "I've just come down."

"Listen, Dato, Señor Manur has just phoned to say that he wants to talk to me and he's coming to see me here in my room, so I won't be able to have breakfast with you and Natalia. Do you have any idea what he might want?"

There was a brief silence and then Dato said:

"Have you committed some error?" I was troubled more by the frankness of his response than by its actual content, that is, the impertinent words "commit" and "error."

"An error? What do you mean? What kind of error?"

Dato fell silent again, long enough for me to ask impatiently:

"Is Natalia with you?"

"She must be just about to come down. Do you want me to ask her to call you?"

"Yes, would you? No, wait; if I can, I'll call her again in a couple of minutes. That would be best."

Just as I hung up, someone knocked at the door, and

I thought it would be Manur. It was the waitress bringing the two breakfasts (coffee and coffee): doubtless Manur had taken the liberty of ordering them before consulting me as to my preferences. While the waitress was placing the trays on the table, I again put a call through to the dining room and this time asked to speak to Señora Manur. I did not know what I was going to say to her, I had no idea. Before leaving, the room service waitress required my signature and—as waitresses always do in luxury hotels to remind the forgetful client of the need for a tip—she smiled rather too broadly: with the telephone in one hand and the cord stretched as far as it would go, I had to fumble for some coins in the pocket of a jacket hanging in the wardrobe. And what I imagine to have been the last of those ten minutes was squandered in useless waiting: when Manur knocked at my door, Natalia Manur had still not come to the phone and I had still not finished shaving. I hung up and went to the door feeling dirty (which I wasn't), ill-dressed (which I wasn't), nervous (which I was) and less than immaculate (which I also was, and you have no idea how it upsets me to be seen when I'm less than immaculate). Manur, on the other hand, was clean and as if new-minted, in his New England-style clothes and smelling of that cologne which might perhaps have aroused feelings of nostalgia in Natalia Manur's passive consciousness. He was carrying his green fedora in his hand, his bald head was impeccable, his moustache neat, and his eyes cold and watchful. He did not say that he had just twenty minutes to spare, nor did he look at his watch. And even before we had done any more than exchange greetings, when he had sat down at the table on which the breakfasts had been laid, when he had poured me a cup of coffee with a steady hand and proceeded to pour one for himself, circumstances conspired once more in his favor. The telephone rang. I picked it up after the first ring hoping it would be that fourth journalist I had erroneously anticipated—even though now it would be too late—and not Natalia Manur. But I was out of luck: what I heard was her voice saying: "Hello, we got cut off. What's wrong? Dato told me to phone you immediately." I had not, I thought, told Dato to tell Natalia Manur to phone me immediately, I had said that I would ring her. I did not know what to say and I had to say something. Manur, in his coffee-colored suit, was already sipping his coffee and, from behind his cup—with his eyes of an entirely different hue—he was watching me intently.

"I can't talk now," I said at last. "I'm sorry, I'll explain later." And I hung up.

"I don't know if that will be possible," Manur was quick to say.

"What do you mean? What won't be possible?"

Manur looked fleetingly at his nails, as I had seen him do before. Then he looked at my still unmade bed, on which lay my electric shaver and the hand mirror. Then he looked at my chin. I almost blushed.

"I see you didn't manage to finish shaving."

"No, you didn't give me enough time."

"Oh, I calculated ten minutes from the time I called you, and, if you don't mind my saying, you do not have a particularly heavy growth of beard." He paused and I thought two things simultaneously: "Manur knows expressions in my language that most foreigners don't" and "Should I ask him now if he's come to talk about my beard and am I supposed to answer to him as to whether or not I've shaved?", but before I had come to any decision, he glanced at the phone, pointed at it with his finger and added: "However, I see that you didn't manage to speak to my wife during those ten minutes either, and I don't know if it will be possible, as I have just told her, for you ever to do so again."

This time I did turn red, and there was no darkness to conceal my blushes.

"I don't understand," I said.

Manur finished his coffee and immediately poured himself another cup. Perhaps he was one of those obsessive drinkers of black coffee, I thought, a voluntary insomniac, a slave to coffee. I still hadn't even tried mine, that is, I still hadn't had any breakfast.

"Nor did you manage to speak to her last night."

I felt a second and much stronger wave of blushes. I thought, though, that perhaps my still unshaven beard might disguise this slightly (I momentarily blessed the fact that I had not finished shaving). I made an awkward attempt to shift my chair slightly so that I was sitting with the light behind me.

"Last night? Of course I spoke to her. I had supper with her and with your secretary, as you doubtless know. We've had supper together nearly every night. We have become good friends."

"That isn't what I meant. I was referring to your phone call to our room at just after half past midnight. Don't you remember? I picked up the phone, and you hung up without saying anything. That's not a nice thing to do at all."

"Ah. And how do you know it was me?"

"I don't want to play games with you. I immediately phoned reception and asked if that fleeting, anonymous call had come from outside or from another room in the hotel, and when they said it had come from another room, I asked them which one."

Again I did not know what to say. I thought: "There seems to be no escape, this man obviously knows what he's doing. It would be best just to own up, to apologize for having phoned so late and invent some excuse." The previous night seemed to me now remote and confused, although I did clearly remember (for they had not gone away) my feelings of desire for Natalia Manur.

"Yes, you're right. I asked for your number because I'd forgotten to tell Natalia something about the performance tonight (which I hope, by the way, you too will be able to attend). Then, when the phone was already ringing, I realized how late it was, which is why I hung up. I'm terribly sorry if I disturbed you, I didn't mean to."

But Manur appeared to have heard only part of my explanation. At every pause, he smiled a minimal, mechanical smile, the same smile with which he had been so prodigal when I was observing him on the train, where he had sat in complete silence, staring straight ahead.

"No," he said, and spread his thick lips into a slightly wider smile, "you hung up afterwards, when you heard my voice." And as if everything else I had said was irrelevant to the conversation, he went on: "Look, it doesn't bother me in the least that my wife should make friends, on the contrary. I'm a busy man and I can't devote all the time to her that I would like, so it seems perfectly normal to me that she should have fun with other people, people like you, for example, an opera singer. However, what I cannot allow is for those other people to demand from her any more than that. In a word, if I see (as I have seen already to be happening with you) that one of those people is beginning to show an excessive or irregular interest in my wife, then I do not hesitate to intervene in order to dissuade that person from continuing. I try, moreover, to do so before any real complications arise, and before the person in question becomes too stubborn or is likely to get hurt, do you understand? That is why I am here now."

I was so surprised that, for a few seconds, I wasn't sure whether it was a bad joke or one of those moments of resounding ingenuousness so often indulged in by northern Europeans, with their incorrigible taste for frankness.

"And what makes you think that I have, as you put it, an excessive and irregular interest in your wife? This all seems somewhat disproportionate to me."

"It's quite simple," said Manur, and with his hand he checked that his green silk tie (which matched his fedora and the paler green of his shirt) was quite straight: he wasn't wearing a tiepin. "It may seem disproportionate to you, but I know that it isn't. Last night, for the first time, you did something anomalous: you phoned at a very late hour and then hung up when you heard my voice. Just one anomalous action is enough for me to see what will happen next. Besides, there was a second anomaly: you had a prostitute sent up to your room, doubtless intending to vent your unease and frustration on her. These two actions of yours last night are intimately linked, and (although it's quite likely that you yourself may not yet have realized it)"—Manur was a pedant—"together they indicate an excessive and irregular interest in my wife. If you haven't realized it yourself, then I am here to put you straight. I know the whole process well and your response is absolutely standard. Believe me, I would prefer to put a stop to it in its initial phases."

I did not blush this time. I thought: "I could deny that link, I could pretend to be insulted and tell him he's mad, but I've got time to do that later; I can also hear what else he has to say."

"You've been extraordinarily quick and efficient in your investigations, Señor Manur. Who told you all this? Céspedes?"—I was pleased that the name came so immediately to mind: in order to instill respect, it is vital to remember the names of both people and things. "Or does Dato keep an eye on me at night as well as during the day?"

"Dato knows nothing about this. I deal personally with any matters affecting my marriage. But I have not yet finished my exposition of the facts. There is a third anomaly: you did not actually avail yourself of the services of that prostitute, did you?"

This Belgian banker knows everything, I thought in some alarm: about my language and about what I did last night. He had even spoken to the prostitute Claudina. But when? Prostitutes tend not to be early risers. Perhaps her next appointment had been with Manur himself. Or would the prostitute have told Céspedes and then Céspedes told Manur? Why would the Argentinian prostitute have let the cat out of the bag like that? Not, of course, that she owed me any loyalty. Besides— and, as I said, this is something I have been thinking about a lot this morning—I had not exactly been very nice to her and had not treated her well. I felt like laughing.

"It seems absurd to me that we should be talking about such things, Señor Manur."

"It would indeed be absurd if, before these things happened, you had not telephoned *my* room. But you did not avail yourself of that prostitute's services,"— Manur repeated this rather formal phrase somewhat hesitantly, as if he had only recently learned it and wanted to try it out—"and I cannot help but interpret this as confirmation of everything I have been saying to you regarding your interest in my wife. We have reached a point when I feel obliged to tell you not to see her again. We will all go to your first night tonight, we will congratulate you after the performance (we will even have a drink afterwards to toast you), but tomorrow you will not meet. In a few days' time, you can bid each other a polite farewell, and she will thank you for your kindness. That shouldn't be so very difficult, since neither you nor we will be spending many more days in Madrid, and I very much hope you will not come to Brussels. I would be most put out."

"Listen, Manur, aren't you getting things out of proportion?"

"Perhaps. But I am allowed to get things out of proportion."

I remained silent for a moment, a moment that Manur deployed to smooth down with one hand his non-existent hair, to finish his second cup of coffee and to pour himself a third, this time from my coffee pot. A slave to coffee. I, on the other hand, had still not drunk mine. I picked up the glass of orange juice (not freshly squeezed) which was on the tray intended for me and held it in one hand without actually raising it to my lips.

"Do you always make Natalia's decisions for her? I imagine she will have her own views on the matter."

"Let's not play games, Mr. Opera Singer," said Manur, and it bothered me that he should address me like that. "At this stage of your friendship with my wife, you must know that our marriage is based on some very unusual conditions. Well, you should know that these conditions, however unfair, are *always* met, as they will be now."

"Most marriages are run like that, at least in theory."

"Not exactly. It is not the case in most marriages that one of the spouses has,"—he paused for a split second—"bought the other, acquired them. My wife belongs to me in the strictest sense of the word 'belong', and that means that what you call her 'views' have only a very relative value."

"Bought? What do you mean?"

For the first time in the conversation, Manur appeared not to have anticipated how I might respond. He raised his eyebrows, a gesture of surprise common to nearly every country I have visited (it seems to be an international gesture).

"Hasn't she told you?"

"She's never spoken to me about you."

"Really?" Manur, I thought, was capable of being quite theatrical. "I don't know whether I should be pleased or worried by that little bit of information. You see, you are not the first man with whom I have had to have such a conversation, you may well not be the last, although my wife is not as young as she was. But the others (believe it or not, there have been quite a few already) were rather better informed. To be honest, I don't quite know what to make of your ignorance. Don't tell me my wife hasn't told you about our marriage! Don't tell me she hasn't complained to you!"— Manur had made an instant recovery from his surprise and now seemed mildly amused. He again straightened his green tie with his hand. He drank more coffee. A tiny drop fell on his tie, but he didn't notice.

"I can assure that she hasn't, no. Besides, Dato has been present at all our meetings. You can ask him."

"I see! That man Dato has gone too far!" exclaimed Manur. And his cognac-colored eyes, and with them all his plebeian features—that is, his expression (that of an actor and a pretender)—underwent an instantaneous transformation and became as grave as those of an animal. Then he went on: "Right then, I'd better explain it to you myself."

"You've spilled a drop of coffee on your tie."

MANUR STARED IN BEWILDERMENT at the tiny drop I was pointing at, my index finger just touching his green tie: the drop was exactly the same color as his coffee-colored suit.

"Do you mind if I use your bathroom?" he asked.

I used the few seconds that Manur remained in my bathroom (he did not even close the door, I could hear the hot water running) to push my chair right back in order to take fullest advantage of the backlighting and to cast a rapid glance at myself in the full-length mirror opposite the beds. Despite my half-shaven chin, I no longer felt quite as dirty or nervous. I saw too that I was not so very badly dressed, and this comforted me.

When Manur came back, he sat down again as if

nothing had happened (nothing had happened, but now there was on his tie a stain left by the water, considerably larger than the drop of coffee) and he began to talk. Everything that he said I heard in this morning's dream exactly as it was spoken then, but, on the other hand, I do not think I could repeat it with the same exactitude, at least not this evening when I am tired and hungry (it's getting dark outside and I still haven't had any lunch and will not have any lunch, but will probably wait until suppertime before I decide whether or not to go out). I can only reproduce fragments of what Manur said, but with the exception of myself shortly afterwards (except I cannot make an exception of myself), I have never seen anyone with such a will to persevere in his choice and in his love. More than that, I now know that it was Manur who infected me, or, rather, that I was the one who exposed myself to contamination or chose to imitate him. For until then, there had been only my desire to go on seeing Natalia Manur every day, my physical desire for Natalia Manur and my desire to destroy Manur. And it was from then on that I began to understand better, in the same way that a man writing can begin to understand what he is writing from one chance phrase that tells him—not suddenly, but slowly—why all the other phrases were as they were, why they were written in that way (which he will see now as having nothing to do with either intention or chance), when he thought he was just feeling his way forward, merely playing with paper and ink to pass the time, because he has been asked to do so or out of the sense of duty felt by all those who have no duty. Have you never discovered in the attitudes or words or gestures of other people what you had never previously been able to put your finger on? Have you never seen in them the brilliance that we ourselves lack, the inconceivable clarity, the firm hand and the assured touch that we will never have, what once was known as "grace." Have you never aspired to be them, precisely because of that transcendent quality, because of their sheer infectiousness, their natural annihilating radiance? Have you never felt the temptation, or more than that, the need scrupulously to copy someone else's being in order to take it from them and appropriate it for yourself? Have you never experienced an uncontrollable desire for usurpation? An unbearable envy at their cheerfulness or their suffering, at their stamina or their will power? At the jealousy felt by another, at their fatalism, their determination or their doom? Who has not wanted to be doomed once and for all and to enjoy the fixity of death in life? Who has not longed to be the object of a curse? Who has not yearned to remain very still and simply to persevere? I am León de Nápóles, the Lion of Naples, and my face is still flushed with triumph: I want to continue being what I am. But I know that it was not always so and that

I did not always have that name. Manur, by his unexpected example, taught me to persevere: Manur persevered in his love. And now, when hunger is gnawing at me, and now that, even though it is spring time, I have had to turn on the light, I see again, as I did four years ago and as I did this morning, his suddenly grave, animal eyes (he said: "I have waited fifteen years to be loved by Natalia Monte, my wife; you, sir, are a mere upstart"), which incomprehensibly did not turn away from the merciless morning light of Madrid pouring in through the window onto his face, lighting it up ("It was purely a business transaction, Natalia's father was facing absolute ruin after years of mismanagement and waste, and his children, Natalia and her brother, Roberto, came to fear that their father might put an end to his depression and his irritability by either shooting himself or shooting his wife, their mother, if his business fortunes did not revive and allow him to return to full activity. He was one of those men for whom activity is everything") and filling his eyes with metallic reflections that made them harder still, although, at one moment, there was just a flicker of grief in them ("It was Roberto's idea, he was the one who persuaded his sister to accept me, and to see that our marriage was an urgent necessity, that an immediate alliance with my family's powerful bank was the only solution; and he personally brought her to Brussels, where, appropriately enough, he was best man at our wedding, since he was, in fact, the one who was giving her away to me. But that was years ago now, far too many years") and that made him look suddenly like his wife, as if not even Natalia and Manur, despite what he was saying, had been able to free themselves entirely from those alarming similarities that time prides itself on developing between those non-blood relatives who are brave enough to see each other every day ("I had met her three months before, when I was on holiday here in Madrid, through her brother, who had done some business courses with me in Brussels; and not only did I court her diligently, I also proposed marriage to her in a last act of desperation dictated by the old-fashioned idea— I had a very conventional upbringing—that her rejections and refusals might be due to the lack of a formal proposal. I have been in love with Natalia Monte, sir, almost since the first moment I saw her"). Those eyes, apparently translucent in the sunlight, cast occasional rapid glances at my unmade bed: there, in desolation, lay my hand mirror and my electric shaver ("I have waited fifteen years for her to love me. And as long as there is no one else, as long as she harbors no hopes and does not love anyone else, I know that I can go on waiting, or at least, year after year, keep to my old plan of spending the rest of my life with her. That is why I will not permit, in anyone, the excessive and irregular interest that you have now begun to show. Most women—and some rather odd men too—love by reflection or, if you prefer, by imitation: they love and desire the other person's love, as has often been shown to be the case and as you yourself will know. That is why I married Natalia Monte and saved her father from absolute ruin and destruction even though I knew this was the only reason she was marrying me, or, rather, because this was the plan of salvation that her brother Roberto had decided upon. And that is also why I have always prevented her from having any other model to inspire her or for her to imitate, any 'other person's love' that might tempt her, and whose existence would constitute—believe me, I'm not lying when I say this—the greatest possible danger for me"); and then invariably, as they had done the first time, his eyes shifted to my chin, reminding me of my abandoned beard and the fact that tonight was the first night of Verdi's *Otello* and that I had still not been able to cover my mouth with sticking plaster—as I usually do on the day of a performance—so that I would be unable to talk during the hours prior to the curtain and could thus nurture and preserve my voice ("For years she was bound to me simply because one word from me or even a signature would have meant returning her calamitous father to the very situation from which she had rescued him by her marriage, or, rather, as I had by mine, by becoming his beloved son-in-law, as wealthy as I was accommodating. Much later, when her father died, followed not long afterwards by her mother, my safeguard was and continues to be Roberto Monte, who is as catastrophic in his business affairs as his father was and to whom my wife is even more devoted"). His thick, pale, fleshy lips moved at extraordinary speed, with his usual fluency in my language, making scarcely a mistake: an unnatural perfection ("Only a few months ago, I had no option but to send him to South America because he was on the point of being arrested and tried here for capital flight, tax evasion and who knows how many other financial misdemeanours. He is my safeguard, sir, and I am perfectly well aware that my wife is anxiously awaiting the moment when her brother Roberto—Roberto rather than I—will release her from her agreement with me by telling her that he is no longer in any danger, that he is no longer dependent on me, that he can fend for himself without fear of reprisals on my part and with no need of my protection. My wife believes that I manipulate things so that this can never happen, and that belief has only helped to fuel her feelings of resentment towards me and become a further obstacle to what I have been waiting for all these years, her wholehearted and unconditional love. In fact, it seems most unlikely that Roberto Monte will ever achieve financial independence or peace, but that will be through no fault of mine: there is no need for me to hinder his plans or to devote myself to laying traps for him: he is perfectly capable of maintaining himself in a permanent state of imminent arrest. But despite that more or less lifelong guarantee, I also require that my wife should have no amatory shadows in her life. You're probably thinking how unhappy she must be, but bear in mind that I am too"). Manur was speaking with great composure and with little show of emotion, but he kept restlessly crossing and uncrossing his legs in a gesture that, in a way, brought him closer to Natalia Manur, as if he had copied it from her or perhaps she from him ("I count for little in her life today, but then there is no one else—nor should there be—who counts for more. I did once count and I will again; and believe me, it will not be long now before she will find herself unable to do without me. For the moment, at least, I see her every day, spend every night in the same bedroom, after my day of work and her day of diversion or self-absorption or perhaps meditation on her own dark fate. But diversion too, don't forget: and that is what we all aspire to, isn't it, to be diverted? I mean, the life she leads would be the envy of many women, not to mention, for example, that prostitute who came to see you last night. Do you think my wife, Natalia Monte, would want to change places with that prostitute? I don't really know that someone in her position has a right to complain, just as I do not consider that someone in my position has a right to complain either. Would I, for example, change places with you?") and while he was talking, he continued pouring and drinking black coffee from the two coffee pots which he had commandeered, until he discovered, with visible annoyance, that there was not a drop of coffee left ("She's a wealthy woman, she has everything she needs—that presents no problem—she has her own bank account which I keep topped up, even a permanent companion whom she likes very much and who seems to keep her amused and with whom she gets on well and to whom she can open her heart whenever she wishes. I don't mind, just as I would not have minded in the least if she had opened her heart to you: I make no secret of any of this, especially not to perfect strangers who will vanish completely from our lives. Why should I care? And if she doesn't have much of a social life, that is because, generally speaking, she prefers not to accompany me to my various suppers and meetings: but that is *her* choice, just as it has been *her* choice not to work, perhaps to punish me with her inactivity. Listen, would you like a little more coffee? These hotels are so cheap with their coffee nowadays"). Then he got up and, after asking me if he could use my phone when he already had it in his hand, he requested— or rather commanded—that more coffee should be brought to my room; then he sat down again, first taking advantage of a fleeting moment in front of the full-length mirror, just as I had done, to cast a rapid glance at his own reflection to check that the water stain and the drop of coffee had both now disappeared. ("You will be wondering what has gone on in our bedroom at night during those fifteen years, but I am not prepared to satisfy your curiosity on that subject. All you need to know is that the conditions on which our marriage is based exclude—independently of what may have happened in the past in our bedroom or what may still happen now—the possibility of our leading separate lives, which is, I believe, the current rather unimaginative euphemism. A failure to meet any one of these conditions would constitute for me a *casus belli* of the most serious kind. As serious as if she were to leave me, do you understand?") On more than one occasion throughout his speech—especially after that Latin tag, I seem to remember—I felt a desire to interrupt him, to ask him a question or to make a point, but his weary, overbearing, alert tone was that of a punctilious, reliable company director whose turn has come to read out a report written with such effort or with such pleasure that he will not allow the members of his board even the most insignificant of interjections or give them the slightest opportunity to object ("You, sir, cannot understand, you will only have experienced ordinary love affairs. The reason I am telling you this is so that you can see exactly what the situation is and what my position is; so that you will know that I am not prepared to let these fifteen years pass by in vain just because of some last-minute slip; so that you will be good enough to leave my wife alone from tomorrow onwards and purge from your thoughts all trace of the excessive and irregular interest of which you gave me ample evidence last night. I am not a neglectful husband. Those who have shared your interest previously have understood this very well: they gauged the obstacles, weighed up the difficulties, saw that it really wasn't worth the effort, gave up and backed off, only once did I have to pay out any money. You should follow their example. Don't complicate my life and don't make things complicated for yourself. Believe me, my wife is not a good deal, not a profitable concern"). When someone knocked at the door and I went to open it, there was not only the waitress bringing more coffee, but also the maid, who, following her own trajectories and her own timetable, had come to make my bed and air the room; Manur, turning round in his chair, invited the former to come in and dismissed the latter ("Come back later, can't you see we're still having breakfast?"), without stopping to think that I might want to have my bed made and my room aired, and to see my beard completely shaven and my mouth covered by the protective strip of sticking plaster reserved for special days like this. While I was signing the

144

tab and paying for the smile, the couple from Cuba or the Canary Islands who were staying in the room next door walked past. They were not early risers. I did not see their faces, only the grey or blue jacket of a suit and a brightly colored dress. She was taller than he was and walked behind him. I caught a whiff of flowery perfume and heard him say "You'll just have to put up with it!" to which she replied "I'm telling you I can't go on like this!" I shut the door and returned to my place, opposite Manur. ("At the moment, you are at a stage when all you have are your thoughts. And what are those thoughts? Nothing, sir, they are so simple that anyone can guess them, so transitory that you can count them as they go by. I can guess yours and you know mine, isn't that so?") Despite having ordered the new coffee with such resolve, Manur did not pour any of it out. Perhaps he had only ordered it so as to give me back the coffee that was due to me and which I had not yet tasted—the coffee he had poured into my cup was now cold—("I will applaud you tonight"). He uncrossed his legs. He got up to go. He stroked his tie. He smoothed his bald head. He picked up his fedora. He looked at his watch ("She smells very good" and I did not know if he was referring to his wife, Natalia Manur, to the woman from Cuba or the Canary Islands who had just walked past and who could not take any more or to Claudina the prostitute, whose cheap, pleasant perfume—the room had still not been aired—might still be perceptible to him). He said:

"Bear in mind that there is no stronger bond than that which binds one to something unreal or, worse, something that has never existed." And I saw him raise his index finger for the third time. That was also the third time that I saw him.

I suppose the fourth journalist finally rang not long afterwards. But by then I had finished shaving and had covered my mouth with sticking plaster: I hesitated for a moment, I did not answer.

I WAS SO HUNGRY THAT I HAD TO pause for a moment and go downstairs to have supper in a nearby restaurant, lively, expensive and crowded, and which, being much frequented by tourists, opens its doors fairly early. First I looked in my mailbox and picked up the letters that had been waiting for me since the morning. No one had brought them up to me because no one has come to see me today. And I've had the answering machine on too, so I haven't seen or spoken to anyone all day, and the day is nearly over. Among various circulars from banks and the odd pre-contract to sing in a couple of years' time at some particular spot on the globe where I know I will be sure to find myself on that precise and distant date, the only letter in the box (and which I read while I was waiting for supper amid the gabble of tourists) was from that man, Noguera, the husband or widower of my girlfriend Berta. Surprisingly—given my silence—he has written to me again, on today of all days, just when Berta had appeared to me again in this morning's dream, only three weeks after I had learned of her death by the same marital route. Noguera, in this second letter, which I have just read, initially goes on again about my old books and warns me that if I do not write to confirm that I want them back, he will have no option but to throw them on the fire along with everything else (that is what he says, "throw them on the fire," an odd expression given that spring is already here). He is not going to continue living in the house or "tower" he shared with Berta, he tells me (and on this occasion, unlike the first, he does mention his state of mind, which is one of despair), because he finds the constant memories of his wife extremely painful. So sadly do the hours pass that he plans not only to leave the marital home, but also to destroy all her belongings and anything that serves to feed her memory, which he intends to allow to "die of inanition." He is still young, he says, he hopes to rebuild his life, and, given that he has the firm intention of destroying photos, clothes, shoes, records, jewelry, lotions, videos, creams, aprons, books, mirrors, pills, letters—in short, everything that his wife ever used while alive—he asks me if, before he lights the pyre, I would like to have—as well as those books of mine that he has already listed—some of those objects which he, "on the other hand," never wants to see again. Perhaps he thinks that, contrary to what is happening to him, I do want to keep Berta's memory alive with something tangible that once belonged to her, and this legalistic individual—whom I now am sure is called Noguera because I have just read his name—sends me another detailed improbable list of all the things he is kind enough to offer me before the planned incineration. Noguera thinks that I would be particularly interested in photos from the time when she and I "saw most of each other" and in the letters and postcards that I sent her ("there are not that many and most are postcards") and which he found in an old tin box of Lindor chocolates. But— he insists—it would be no trouble at all to send me any other object I might like to keep. If, within two weeks, he receives no answer—just as he received no answer to his first letter—he will assume that I have no desire to keep anything "from the above inventory" and he will proceed with the "cremation," which is why, if there is anything I want, he urges me to reply and gives me his Barcelona telephone number in case my many travels and commitments ("which I know about from the newspapers and the television") do not leave me enough time to write and it would be easier for me to tell him over the phone what I would like to keep. I have not dared to read the new list closely, it is several pages long, but when I glanced over it—repeatedly in fact— I noticed two things: that Noguera is mad enough to include in it all kinds of things that have nothing whatever to do with me, things clearly bought long after I had ceased to have anything to do with Berta; but he is not mad enough to offer me (as I had begun to fear) tights and panties and other such things—which will doubtless be among the objects to be devoured by the fire—nor her set of silver cutlery, her record player, her video machine or her television—which will certainly not be consumed by the flames in a fortnight's time. Noguera, unhinged by the unexpected and possibly avoidable death of his wife (and it is perfectly normal that he should be more troubled now than the first time he wrote to me, when he had just buried her and when the sense of calm and reason that the dead bestow on us would not yet have deserted him), is incapable of understanding that if *he* wants to forget Berta Viella, then *no one else* will want to remember her. For the last person is the one who counts, thus, for example, it will be our last widow who will have to be consoled, and any inheritance we leave will almost always go to those who did not know us when we were young, but only when we were already deep in vile decrepitude or in rigid old age. That is why neither I nor anyone else in the world considers the great Gustav Hörbiger to be the most heroic Heldentenor of our century, but, rather, an obsessed madman, doubtless confined in some German hospital and whose imminent death will not now be his defining moment. That is why Otello is an avenger and Liu a martyr until the end of time, that is why I cannot easily forget Manur (that is why, on the other hand, I do not yet know what I am nor if anyone or no one will remember me). Noguera, with his impossible offer, is trying to contravene an immutable law, according to which the last person is the one who determines, sanctions, amends or cancels everything that came before. He is and always will be Berta's husband, her final choice, and if he now regrets and is wearied by his inability to forget, what he cannot do is to try and carry out an illicit transfer and pass that responsibility over to me. I cannot perform an act of palingenesis, I do not want to remember her; more than that, as I said before, I do not remember her now. I don't want those books that were once mine, I don't want her photos of monuments and faces and beaches, nor the postcards I sent to her from half the known world, I don't want a sponge or a bathrobe, or a scratched record of Lauritz Melchior or even a new one by Pavarotti, let alone one of me singing sublime extracts from seven operas. I don't want her medicines or her sunglasses, her stiletto heels or her azaleas; her random selection of novels, her rings, her colorful earrings, her unopened bottles of Rhine wine and Veuve Clicquot; her cologne, her eye drops, her lamps, her lipsticks, her bits of pottery from La Bisbal, the trilobite I gave her; her silk-blend blouses, her glass Murano ashtrays, her iridescent skirts, her shells from the Lido, her English teapots, her collection of cockerels from around the world and made of all kinds of materials, her—very lovely—Fortuny engravings. I do not want anything that she once owned. Or perhaps just one thing: because although I had no intention of doing so, between courses—the restaurant was so crowded, the waiters so rushed, the hubbub of voices so loud that even the normally affable head waiter did not speak to me, and, unable to eavesdrop on anyone else's conversation, I grew bored—I spent rather too much time leafing through the mad, meticulous sheets that Noguera had sent me, and on the third page, I noticed this object, "elegant Italian calendar" (that is the description given by poor Noguera, about whom I still know nothing, what he does or who he really is). I wonder if it is the same one (*marzo, ottobre, dicembre*) that adorned the bedroom wall in our apartment in Barcelona, I mean, I wonder if it is the same make or the same series, if the very precise Berta would have continued buying them all these years and if they were therefore still being made. I could ask Noguera to send me that elegant calendar. Besides, in a few months' time it will be out of date and will have to be thrown out anyway, it will not last nor will it remind me for very long of what I am now incapable of remembering. Perhaps it would do me good to look at it during that time, for I fear that, from now on, no one will watch over my sleep nor will I watch over that of Natalia Manur. This morning, when I woke, she was not in our vast bed with its four lion's feet and she has still not come home. There may be nothing strange about this. I have slept so badly and so little for so many years that I now take a powerful soporific (twenty-five drops) that plunges me into such a deep torpor that until I have had my eight hours of sleep nothing can wake me apart, that is, from my own will, alerted before I drop off, or else another person's will to interrupt my slumbers and return me to the world: on occasions when Natalia needed me during the night, she had to call out my name and shake me and unbutton my pajama jacket and splash cold water on my forehead and neck. But last night, my thoughts were not vigilant, and she clearly did not need me, so she must have gone out early without my noticing and, quite possibly, she was in a hurry, so much so that she did not even leave me a note explaining where she was going or at least warning me that she would not be back for lunch or supper. Yes, she was probably in a hurry, because she seems to have gone off somewhere on a trip—it's impossible to know if she went by plane or train—and when one is traveling, there is never time to spare. Two expandable suitcases and a large bag are missing from the wardrobe where we keep our luggage, as are most of her more personal belongings, of which I would not now be able to make a list like Noguera's because, unlike him, I do not have them here before me. However she has taken with her the things one never leaves behind: almost nothing of hers remains in the bathroom and my toothbrush is alone again, as it was once before; I know that her drawers are now empty of her underwear and her wardrobes of her autumn clothes, which leads me to think—given that, in our hemisphere, spring is just beginning—that perhaps she has flown off to Argentina, the country where her brother Roberto (whom, it is true, she has not seen for a long time and whom she often misses) enjoys a prosperous lifestyle and where he has chosen to remain. Yes, perhaps, on an impulse, she decided to go and see him. But an impulse like that requires planning, and there is also the possibility that Natalia Manur has simply left me without saying a word, as she left Manur four years ago, about which I also dreamed this morning. (Natalia has so often told me how she used to say to him: "When I do finally leave, you won't even know.") During the last few weeks or possibly months (time is so slippery when one is constantly on the move and, during the years that we have lived together, my profession has meant that we have traveled the world together), she seemed tired of so much to-ing and fro-ing and tired too—just a little—of me. She had again developed those dark shadows under her eyes that only accentuate her femininity, and she laughed less than she used to, revealing the beautiful teeth that light up her face, and—an old habit acquired in early youth, or perhaps only in Brussels—she had resumed that furious gnawing of the skin around her nails, so that her two index fingers—especially those, but the others as well—had again taken on the ugly, childish, raw appearance they had had during our time in Madrid. But what worried me most was the abnormal weariness that overwhelmed her whenever we arrived in a new place where I was to sing. Something which, only four, three or two years ago, or even six months ago, was for her a source of the greatest pleasure seemed to have become a torment borne without any violent complaint, indeed with hardly any complaint at all, but borne—of this I am sure—with great suffering. On our last few trips, she did not even have the strength to unpack the suitcases: she still withstood the departure well and appeared completely composed and even cheerful during the extreme provisionality of the journeys themselves; however, once the bellboy had shown us to our room, she experienced a kind of invincible exhaustion and collapsed, as if felled by lightning, onto one of the beds in the hotel room. After a couple of hours lying there,

dazed or in a light sleep, she gathered together suffi-
cient strength to get undressed and take a shower; then
she would lie down again and thus, alternating showers
and siestas and a bit of reading or television, she would
remain for the whole of our stay in whatever city we
happened to be in. She no longer wanted to sally forth
on her own to visit places (even though we had recently
been to Prague, Paris and Berlin) nor attend my rehearsals (even though I had lately performed such
highly prestigious roles as Aeneas and Pinkerton and
Des Grieux) nor to pick me up afterwards to go and
have supper in the company of illustrious colleagues
and interesting people (even though we had recently
coincided with Anna Telesca and with the picturesque
Guillerme and the handsome Jerusalem). She asked for
her meals to be taken up to her room, she insisted on
speaking and hearing only Spanish and, in short, she
passed through those cities—which not long ago she
had been thrilled to visit and in which she had eagerly
tracked down all kinds of ornaments and implements
for our home—as if she only existed as a name on a
plane ticket. She behaved like a character in an excellent
comedy I saw recently on video, about a delightful ex-
boxer, fat, loyal and punch-drunk, who had no idea
whether he was in Chicago, New Orleans or Detroit,
so accustomed had he become in his previous pugilistic
life to enforced confinement to his hotel room. I don't

know what Natalia did while I was rehearsing the opera or recording the record that had taken us to wherever we were, but during the brief moments on recent trips when we were together in the room, she just used to lie on the bed—often swathed in a bath towel because she didn't have the energy to get dressed again after a shower—reading all kinds of magazines or dozing or, at the least, yawning, and—the television always on, albeit on mute so as not to disrupt my studies or my practice or because she wasn't interested anyway or didn't want to hear another language—responding only in mono-syllables to my comments or attempts at conversation and proffering only her cheek or her forehead in response to my displays of affection. In a couple of cities, a propos of nothing, she suddenly wondered out loud, in an almost nostalgic tone of voice, what had become of Dato, and the truth is that she no longer seemed to take the same pleasure in my voice or my singing: indeed I had seen her look distinctly bored—even pull a face—when I was doing my vocal exercises in her pres-ence and had just performed a few vertiginous vibratos or stentorean tremolos, which once would have pro-voked her astonishment. In Paris and Berlin, she claimed to have a migraine and did not even attend my performances. She had never missed one before. And she did not seem a great deal happier in the brief peri-ods we spent at home. But it was not until this morning, when I woke from my dream with the renewed image of the one moment (as I have already described to you) when her face appeared to me with utter clarity, when I realized that the look on her face in recent times, the non-expression that predominated when she was lying down, leafing through magazines or half-watching TV programs or, at most, standing at the window and gazing impassively down at a beautiful avenue or a historic square or an ancient church or at a country's enigmatic inhabitants transformed into articulated miniatures, was the same one I had seen that first time and which had made me realize that Natalia Manur (when I still did not know her name) was afflicted by—how did I put it?—a form of melancholy dissolution.

AND IT IS ALL OF THIS, WHAT happened four years ago in reality and in this morning's true and ordered dream, which I am still able to recall and which I cannot now stop myself recalling, because not enough time has passed as yet. What else happened? Or what else did I dream, as the dream grows more distant and more diffuse as I write? Ah, yes, I dreamed that I was kissing Natalia Manur for the first time, almost without knowing I was, in that other (non-luxury) hotel room to which we went on the afternoon following the first night of Verdi's *Otello* in the Teatro de la Zarzuela, when Manur's prohibition order was already in force and when Manur had already been abandoned by Natalia, although he did not know it then. Nor did I: most of the time one does not know when one has been taken up and when one has been abandoned, not just because this always happens behind one's back, but because it is impossible to pinpoint the moment when such upheavals happen, just as one never knows if the fact of being taken up has to do with one's own merits or virtues, one's own unrepeatable existence, one's own decisive intervention or, rather, merely to one's casual insertion into another person's life. I have never had any real sense, in all this time (in the interval between exclaiming "Now is my time!" and saying "Our time is over!"—the interval taken up by these last four years), of having played a personal, unequivocal, vital part in Natalia Manur's decision—after fifteen years of acceptance of and submission to an enforced situation, after fifteen years of a coexistence built on routine, on certain agreed conditions, on an economic pact, on a fear of reprisals and on the abolition of her previous life, on waiting and perhaps, too, on a mutual love that went unrecognized, in every sense of the word—to put an end to that situation and to that coexistence one afternoon in the middle of May and to go on to create a substitute based on far less solid and binding things: freedom of choice, a persuasive argument, the adulation of love, a few ardent kisses, defiance, expectation and perhaps, too, a passion as recognizable as it was primitive. I don't know if the determining factor was that I was the fifth or tenth or fifteenth of the suitors who had been tyrannically and abusively driven away by her husband (the suitor whom it was ordained would provoke a cry of "Enough!") or if it was the absence from Madrid of Roberto Monte—experienced for the first time—that made her lose all patience and forget all about her fears for her brother and for herself and to perceive what remained of her future as blacker now than she had ever known it when she still had so much future left: five, ten or even fifteen more years, since the beginning of her marriage. I only know that at the end of the long-awaited first night of Verdi's *Otello*, and contrary to what Manur himself had said, neither he nor she nor Dato came to my dressing-room to congratulate me and later celebrate my success with me. Claudina the prostitute did not come either, or her sponsor, Céspedes: they were, after all, some of the very few people whom I knew in Madrid at the time, even though it had been the city of my adolescence, but, as I have said, I neglected, alas, to invite them. As I have also said, my godfather, Señor Casaldáliga, to whom I sent two tickets by motorcycle messenger, did not come either. I gave the rest of my quota to the Heldentenor Otello, who—for he was still pretending to possible rivals that everything was perfectly normal—had asked me more than once if, by any chance, I had tickets to spare, so numerous were his social commitments. No one knocked at my dressing-room door, that is, no one who should have knocked as opposed to those who knocked spontaneously, and I was not, therefore, able to spend that night with the people who had—one might say—unceasingly kept me company in Madrid. When it was confirmed to me that everyone in the audience had left the theater, I found myself dragged off by my colleagues and by the impresarios (always eager to be seen with the stars, and I was on my way to becoming a star) to a late supper in a noisy restaurant and then to one of those tumultuous café terraces where, as soon as the good weather arrives, the natives of Madrid love to linger after one of their many walks. My most vivid memory of that evening is the continual passing—as happens anywhere in Madrid and at any time after sunset—of the scrupulous garbage trucks: every few moments, a terrible racket and the stink of rubbish would ruin both one's conversation and the taste of one's drink. I think now that I only put up with being in those places and with those people for so long because it comforted me not to know what had happened between the Manurs (that blissful state of uncertainty) and because I was afraid I would find out if I went back to the hotel, where, perhaps, I might be told what I already suspected and what I definitely did not want to hear: that they had vanished without trace. It was a ghastly night. Desdemona or the lovely Priés had brought with her the clumsy and ill-favored (Spanish) first violin from the orchestra and—doubtless feeling bolder and more empowered after her clamorous triumph on stage—she brazenly showered him with wet kisses and absentmindedly stroked his hairy chest. Fortunately, Iago or the fatuous Volte, left fairly early, because, although the next day was one of complete rest, he was hoping to spend the morning perfecting (that's the word he used—"perfezionare") certain aspects of his interpretation; however, before leaving, he pontificated for ten minutes on the limitations of my performance. Otello or Hörbiger got slightly drunk, told mischievous anecdotes and more or less demanded to be listened to by everyone present at that large table (fifteen or twenty people, of whom almost no one understood German, the only language he could speak coherently and fluently when in that state): now and then—so I was told—he would bawl out in his own language from the head of the table: "Listen, listen, everyone, this is really funny!"; his worst enemy, however, was not linguistic incomprehension, but the city's obsessive and tyrannical rubbish collection system and its ubiquitous trucks which kept drowning out everything. It was after one such pestilential blast, immediately followed by the usual hideous grinding noises, that, quite without warning, I was sick on the sandy ground of the café terrace. Now vomiting, but more especially retching, is disastrous for a singer. There was a moment of general alarm, and nearly everyone—either out of disgust or fear that they themselves might feel sick—turned their back on me. I cleaned myself up as best I could with my own handkerchief and with another that someone lent me, and, when I was feeling slightly better, I took a taxi back to the hotel, where a message awaited me, presented in person by Céspedes (who was clearly on permanent night duty) along with my key. I saw that he had noticed my stained jacket, but he made no comment about this or about my waste, the previous night, of his staff masseuse, about which I assume he knew. He merely asked, in his professional tones, if I needed anything before going to bed.

The note was from Dato, who asked me to go to his room without fail, as soon as I got back to the hotel, regardless of the lateness of the hour. It was half past two and I was utterly exhausted, and the benefits of uncertainty had run their course: now I needed to know, and so I went up to Dato's room. I have rarely seen a man in such a state of contained anxiety as Dato, the former stockbroker with the eighteenth-century hands, in the early hours of that morning. He had been smoking while he waited for me—the ashtray was overflowing— and he was wearing a burgundy red silk dressing gown, although underneath he still had on his shirt and trousers; he had shoes on too, brown shoes (with laces). He looked me up and down several times, doubtless because I was looking absolutely terrible. But it was also as if he were looking at me for the first time and with new eyes, perhaps as I imagine I would have looked at Noguera four years ago if he had been introduced to me then as the future husband of my girlfriend Berta.

"I trust you will turn up in a more presentable state for the rendezvous I have been asked to make for you tomorrow morning. Would you like something to drink?" And with that, he placed one hand on the handle of the small fridge or minibar in his room. He didn't even give me time to shake my head. "No, I suspect not, given your condition. Some mishap?"

I looked down at my jacket.

"I didn't have a chance to change, but it was nothing very serious. What's wrong?"

"You probably know that better than I do. It looks as if you're going to relieve me completely of my role as companion, perhaps deprive me of a job as well." The man speaking was no longer the indispensable and circumspect Dato, the silent presence at our suppers and conversations and walks and shopping expeditions, he was once again the man I had met on his own in the hotel bar: lively, frivolous, disrespectful, although now he was not smiling (he was simultaneously vivacious and somber).

"What do you mean? What are you talking about? Why weren't you all there at the theater?"

Dato lit another cigarette and immediately tapped it with one finger to get rid of some as yet non-existent ash. He was agitated, but, as I said, still very contained.

"I don't know, not that it matters. I have no idea what's going on, for the first time in many years, I simply don't know. But don't concern yourself on my account, there's no real danger of my losing my job. On the contrary, I will probably prove to be even more essential, now I'll just have the other half to take care of. As I told you once before, dealing with a married couple is like dealing with one very contradictory and forgetful person. Now it will be different, perhaps easier, a man alone and without contradictions," and he said again: "a man alone."

I said nothing. Dato was smoking. Suddenly, his face lit up (slightly) and his protuberant gums appeared:

"Unless, of course, I am wrong to assume that I know what your intentions are. If tomorrow, when you go to your rendezvous, you merely have a bit of fun, enjoy yourself and then leave things as they are, as they have always been...that, if you will allow me, is what I would recommend. It would be for the best, not perhaps for Natalia or for you, but certainly for me and for Señor Manur. And probably for the two of you as well, although I doubt that you'll believe me."

"What appointment are you talking about? Can you just tell me what you're talking about? Where's Natalia?"

On this occasion, despite once again making the mistake of asking more than one question at a time, Dato answered all of them.

"Natalia is in her room, sleeping with Señor Manur. The reason I asked you to come and see me is to give you a message from her. She told me to reserve a room in this hotel," as he spoke, he picked up a card from the table with two fingers and handed it to me, "and she wants you to go there with her at five o'clock tomorrow afternoon. She won't be able to see you before, I mean, at breakfast and everything. I presume it is a romantic assignation," and he did not make the slightest pause between this comment and what he went on to say, as if he wanted his first comment to be heard, but to go unnoticed. "She also told me to congratulate you on your performance tonight. She is sure, she says, that it was a great success. She is very sorry that she could not be there."

I looked at the name and address of the hotel. It was in the same street, almost opposite I seemed to remember—a modest place, as if it had been the first one that Natalia Manur had seen when she walked out of our hotel.

"Thank you," I said. Then I hesitated: "Listen, Dato, I assume Señor Manur doesn't know anything about this."

Dato stubbed out his cigarette without finishing it, with an air of irritation and with a despair that was still new.

"What do you think? You spoke to him this morning, you met him, didn't you? That had never happened before."

"What had never happened before?"

"I told you that Natalia Manur had no lovers."

Before Dato I was incapable of blushing.

"You told me that you only kept Señor Manur informed of what you knew and nothing else, and that you didn't know if she had or had ever had any lovers. Tomorrow, on the other hand," I still did not blush, "tomorrow she might have a lover, about whom you will be informed. I don't know if you intend telling Manur, but it seems to me that, with a man like him, there is a great difference between telling him before and telling him afterwards."

Dato took his pack of cigarettes out of his dressing gown pocket and, with those slenderest of fingers, which looked as flammable as the paper or the match, he lit another one.

"My dear sir, you don't seem to understand, or perhaps you are actually going to do what I have advised you to do, but which I am assuming you won't. If Natalia Manur goes to that rendezvous tomorrow and you go too, if you do not restrict yourself, as I have suggested, to having a bit of fun and being more or less satisfied with that, then there will be no need for me to say anything that night to Señor Manur. She won't come back and he will know that she won't come back. I don't know at what point in the small hours he will give in and admit it (that is when he will come to me), but he will have understood before day breaks. It is only right that this time, when it is for real, that she should not have to put up with his scenes. I will do that." He fell silent for a moment and breathed the smoke from his cigarette out through his nostrils, as if he were trying to disguise a sigh. Then he said: "Don't you see? You have been chosen."

I have heard nothing more of Dato since that stay in Madrid, I have not even been able to imagine his face during the four years that have passed between the events I am recounting and this morning. Today I can see him clearly again, although I know that, over the next few days, his mysterious, ageless features will inevitably fade again. I can clearly see his curly hair and his bulging eyes, his tiny hands and his rubbery gums, his lace-up shoes and his burgundy red silk dressing gown (I can see especially those minute hands that will no longer pick up the change from bills paid for by his mistress, and, who knows, perhaps it was the very disinterestedness of that gesture that tipped the balance in her favor at that point). I can see too his scornful expression when, as I was leaving the room and turned to ask him why he did not try to stop that rendezvous, that inauguration, why he favored Natalia Manur over her husband, he replied in a hoarse, rusty voice, half-concealed by a mouthful of unexhaled smoke:

"It's hard to know whom one favors by an action or by an omission, but one can also tire of having no preferences at all."

Just as that was the last time I heard Dato speak, so five o'clock in the afternoon of the following day was the first time that I saw Natalia Manur without her companion, who—obedient, venal, divided, but also subject to his choices—did not, in fact, follow us that afternoon of green- and orange-tinged clouds and high winds, when Natalia Manur and I walked into the rented room in that rather sordid hotel because we had nowhere else to go in the city which had once been both hers and mine. I closed the door and, with silent ardor, almost without knowing I was doing so, rained down kisses upon her face, as if I were in a hurry to touch her soul. I kissed her pale cheeks, her firm forehead, her heavy eyelids, her large, pale lips. And, almost without knowing what was happening, she felt herself lifted up by my powerful embrace, as if I were launching a wave over her head which would overwhelm her with its mere passing.

WHEN YOU DIE, I WILL TRULY mourn you. I will approach your transfigured face to plant desperate kisses on your lips in one last effort, full of arrogance and faith, to return you to the world that has rendered you redundant. I will feel that my own life bears a wound and will consider my own history to have split in two by that final, definitive moment of yours. I will tenderly close your surprised, reluctant eyes and I will watch over your white, mutant body all through the night and into the pointless dawn that will never have known you. I will remove your pillow and the damp sheets. Incapable of conceiving of life without your daily presence and seeing you lying there, lifeless, I will want to rush headlong after you. I will visit your tomb and, alone in the cemetery, having climbed up the steep hill and having looked at you, lovingly, wearily, through the inscribed stone, I will talk to you. I will see my own death foretold in yours, I will look at my own photo and, recognizing myself in your stiff features, I will cease to believe in the reality of your extinction because it gives body and credibility to my own. For no one is capable of imagining their own death.

Manur waited four days before beginning to die, that is, before trying to kill himself with the gun that he owned and which he dared to carry with him over borders when he crossed them by train; and that was the only time—until today—when I ran the risk of losing Natalia Manur and had to beg her in that hotel room and say to her, as I did in my dream: "I do not want to die like a fool." But she wanted to be by his side while he was recovering and she did, in fact, return to his side and was with him during the three weeks that it took for him not to recover, but to die. That at first apparently failed attempt took place while I was on stage at the Teatro de la Zarzuela playing the role of Cassio in Verdi's *Otello* for the third and last time in Madrid and while Natalia was gazing admiringly up at me from her seat in the packed stalls. When we found out, on returning very late from our private celebration, Manur was already sleeping in a hospital and everything seemed to indicate that he would live. They had found him five hours earlier, immediately after the shot was fired: a couple—possibly the couple from Cuba or the Canary Islands—got out on the wrong floor: they had been playing on the elevators after consuming a variety of cocktails in the bar downstairs. The woman, who had the key in her handbag, tried in vain to open the door to what they believed to be their room; he, impatient with what he took to be either her excessive clumsiness or some new jape on her part, grabbed the key from her and, in the midst of their giggles and their fruitless grappling with the door to Manur's room, they were startled to hear the clear sound of a gunshot inside. Alerted by the couple, the night porter in turn informed the manager, who arrived at the door bearing the pass key and accompanied by three assistants. Also present was Dato, who had been notified at once. This group could do nothing to prevent the tipsy couple following in their footsteps in the midst of loud exclamations and guffaws of laughter. After knocking and receiving no reply, they opened the door and went inside, where they found Manur on the floor at the foot of an armchair, from which he had doubtless fallen after the impact. He was sitting with his back against the edge of the seat, the tails of his jacket all rumpled. The breeze was buffeting the net curtains, which looked blue in the early evening dark. One light was on, in the bathroom, projecting an illuminated rectangle onto the floor. Manur was not inside that rectangle. He was dressed as if to go out. He was wearing the glasses which, earlier, I had not been sure he would wear or not. He had the gun in his hand—his index finger still on the trigger— and a hole in his chest. Blood was soaking his shirt, jacket and tie. Like a traveling salesman.

His hand had wavered and the bullet intended for his heart had pierced his left lung instead, without harming any vital organ. Unless, of course, his hand had held firm and he had wounded what he meant to wound, although, in that case, he ran the risk of a fatal deviation. They thought at first that Manur would live, but this did not turn out to be the case. I know nothing about medicine or wounds or weapons or bullets (indeed, I understand almost nothing outside my own profession), but it was explained to me that not only are bullets usually dirty—bullets *are* dirty, it seems—but they carry with them as they enter the body the fragment of clothing which they pierce and drive inwards, and clothing always contains bacteria which, if the doctor in charge of the operation is not sufficiently skilled and conscientious or is simply unlucky, can produce extremely serious infections which sometimes prove fatal: and that is all Natalia said when she told me later what had happened to Manur. (Perhaps, if he had not taken pains to keep his tie straight at the moment he fired the shot, the fragment of cloth that penetrated his lung, causing the fatal infection, could have come from the green tie onto which, in my presence, he had spilled a drop of coffee a few days before, but it is impossible to know whether it was or not, because no one will now remember—if, indeed, anyone noticed—what exactly he was wearing when he shot himself; it also occurs to me that perhaps Manur wanted to die, not immediately but with Natalia by his side—the incarnation of his life—and that he had not missed the target at all, but had aimed accurately, having taken care beforehand, however, to make sure that the bullet was dirty: who knows, perhaps he had conscientiously soiled and smeared it the previous night with rubbish from some trashcan he had walked past before the insatiable garbage trucks of the city of Madrid began their devouring work.) He died, as I said, three weeks after the attempt (which at that point, I suppose, ceased to be an attempt) and Natalia Manur was by his side until the last moment. (She saw him die and has never spoken to me about his death or about those three weeks, of which I know nothing.) I cancelled a song recital in Lisbon programmed for some days later and returned to Barcelona two days after that shot was fired in the luxury hotel bedroom or—which comes to the same thing—the morning after Natalia had abandoned our second hotel, in which, therefore, if I am not mistaken, I spent only one night without her. (I think I felt that I should start preparing Berta for when—once Manur had either recovered or died—Natalia decided to come looking for me again and returned to my side. But that thought did not appear in my dream.)

I did not see him, I mean, I did not see Manur bloodied or bandaged or convalescent or dying. Nor, of course, did I see him dead. I have always believed that he made a mistake, that despotic man who, at first sight, seemed incapable of making mistakes and nevertheless made so many. I don't know what that mistake was, though, and I only, in fact, know what Dato told Natalia and what she told me: that Manur spent the first three days of his solitude carrying out, unaltered, the activities he had planned before his discovery on the night (or perhaps the dawn) following my première. According to Dato, he reacted very calmly at first, contrary to what one would expect and contrary to how he usually reacted to such alarms, false or at least foreseeable. He did not even try to get his secretary to tell him where we were meeting, which was, of course, almost immediately opposite his hotel. Dato said—so Natalia told me—that he seemed absorbed, almost indifferent and, above all, showed not the slightest desire to talk about her departure, nor even to complain. Dato did say, however (though Dato might have been lying about this and about everything, as anyone might when recounting something that only he knows or claims to know), that the only strange behavior he noticed was that, on two of those evenings, Manur turned on the television and watched for a long time, something unheard-of in a man as restless and active as Señor Manur (he watched a game show and a soccer match involving Real Madrid). The evening or night on which he attempted to kill himself and indeed later succeeded in doing so was preceded by a normal working day—

which, in his case, meant a day of intense activity—nor did he make any special arrangements or try to resolve all the things that had taken him to Madrid in the first place. There were still many matters pending and he had even made two appointments for the following morning, in theory, the penultimate day of his stay in the city. There was absolutely nothing—Dato said—in the previous seventy-two hours or on the actual day of the attempt that would have indicated to anyone what his intentions were. He may not have had any intentions. Manur may have returned to his room as the day was beginning to draw to a close and, worn out, he may have lain down, fully clothed, on the double bed, having first placed his green fedora on the bedspread beside him, doubtless unaware of the superstition that says that you should never put your hat down on the bed. It may be that after lying down for ten or fifteen minutes, he picked up the remote control and watched television alone, as I used to watch it with Berta when I came back to Barcelona from one of my trips and as, in recent weeks, Natalia had endlessly done in our latest luxury rooms in the great capitals of the world where I was singing. It may be that on that evening or night there were no game shows or soccer matches. It may be that Manur then got up and opened the wardrobe in order to change his clothes or to put on a dressing gown which, like Dato's, would be made of silk, but, unlike the one I saw Dato wearing, it would probably be coffee-colored or green, Señor Manur's favorite colors, at least according to the indelible image or idea of him I have been left with. But perhaps he did not get as far as changing his clothes or putting on that dressing gown, because in that wardrobe he would have seen, as I saw today in the wardrobes here, many of the clothes left behind by Natalia Manur, who arrived in the second, sordid hotel immediately opposite with only the bare essentials in the medium-sized, expandable suitcase which, for four days, I saw lying on the floor of our room and which she still owns and which she took away with her this morning. Perhaps Manur would have touched those clothes with his slightly plump fingers, he would probably have kissed them with his thick lips or have rubbed his coarse features against the per-fumed, lifeless material, and a slight growth of beard (he will have to shave again tonight, if he intends going out) prevents the material from sliding smoothly over his cheeks. Manur watches the evening fall: he opens the balcony door so that he can get a better view of pre-cisely how the evening falls, and a spring-like air, unlike that in his own country, slightly stirs the net curtains which the darkness has not yet tinged with blue and which would have been identical to those I had in my room, although I, on the other hand, did not have a double bed, but two singles with a rug between them.

Manur puts on his glasses and turns to glance at the television which has nothing of interest to offer him; then he looks outside again: the Madrid sky, a plane in which I will no longer be afraid to fly, the street, the square, the women going out all dressed up, the cars in their many colors. This is not his country. His cognac-colored eyes stare out calmly and deliberately through his glasses: they no longer skim rapidly over or feel flattered by the things of the world. Manur turns off the television and switches on the light in the bathroom, in whose mirror he catches a fleeting glimpse of himself—his robust self—but he does not stop. He smoothes his few hairs without realizing that he is doing so. He urinates with the door open, he still has his jacket on. He goes back into the room, he watches the evening as it falls. He sits down and waits for night to come. He does not smell of anything. My day is over and I feel sleepy, I wonder what I will dream about tonight when I put down this pen and go to bed alone. My consciousness is accustomed to remaining alert (*gennaio, agosto, novembre*). Manur looks at his hand in the shadows. Then, sitting down, dressed to go out, he feels a desire to destroy himself. My hand is in the shadows. But don't worry, I would be incapable of following his example.

Epilogue: Something Unfulfilled

The Man of Feeling has its origins in two images: the first could well belong not so much to the real world as to an illustrated edition of *Wuthering Heights* or to one of the film versions made of Emily Brontë's novel. The image depicts a man and a woman standing in a rural landscape and separated by a fence. They are talking, perhaps having just met, or perhaps saying goodbye. This image, however, does not appear in my book; it served only as a stimulus, it was—to use Nabokov's expression—its first throb. The second image is drawn from the real world and is there in the early part of the book: traveling by train from Milan to Venice, I spent three hours sitting opposite a woman who corresponded exactly to the moral and physical description that the reader will find a few pages into the book. When I started writing the novel, that was almost all I had, that and the opening sentence.

This is how I usually work. I need to feel my way forwards, and nothing would bore me or put me off more than knowing, when I start a novel, precisely what it will be: the characters who will people it, when and how they will appear or disappear, what will become of their lives or of the fragment of their lives that I am going to recount. All this happens as I am actually writing the novel and belongs to the realm of *invention* in its etymological sense of discovering or stumbling upon something; there are even moments when I stop and see opening up before me two possible, and totally opposed, ways of continuing the story. Once the book is finished—that is, once the discovery has been made, and once the book *exists* in the particular way that publication makes immutable—it seems impossible that it could ever have been any different. Then one *believes* that one can talk about it, even explain it, using other words than those used in the book itself, as if those words were not suitable for all circumstances.

The Man of Feeling is a love story in which love is neither seen nor experienced, but announced and remembered. Can such a thing happen? Can something as urgent and unpostponable as love, which requires both presence and immediate consummation or consumption, be announced when it does not yet exist or truly remembered if it no longer exists? Or does the announcement itself and mere memory—*now* and *still* respectively—form part of that love? I don't know, but I do believe that love is based in large measure on its anticipation and on its recollection. It is the feeling that requires the largest dose of imagination, not only when one senses its presence, when one sees it coming, and not only when the person who has experienced and lost love feels a need to explain it to him or herself, but also while that love is evolving and is in full flow. Let us say it is a feeling which always demands an element of fiction beyond that afforded by reality. In other words, love always has an imaginary side to it, however tangible or real we believe it to be at any given moment. It is always about to be fulfilled, it is the realm of what might be. Or, rather, of what might have been.

This is the realm inhabited by the characters in *The Man of Feeling*: we are witnesses to those fragments of their stories during which—through anticipation or memory—they are obliged to live with love either when they do not yet have it or when they have already lost it. The difference between the two principal male characters lies in the fact that while one of them is not prepared to make do with that imaginary, projected, fictitious dimension, and takes the necessary steps to replace the love only glimpsed with a love lived (to have his love fulfilled), the other character, the true man of feeling, has accepted—patiently, though not resignedly—that imaginary, unilateral route and has staked his life on it. To the former, the end of his love will not prove so very terrible—as, indeed, is the case for most people in present-day society—because from the moment he chooses reality, or, if you prefer, fulfilment, he has automatically chosen the point of view of memory, which makes all things bearable. However, when the other man loses his unfulfilled love (as he perceives it), he is forced to abandon the true realm of love, that of possibility and the imagination. And it is that loss, above all, that drives him to despair.

In the middle is a female character, Natalia Manur, who is shown in the novel in a very diffuse way, as if through a veil. She is only seen clearly on one occasion, at the start of the book, asleep, just as I saw that woman on the Milan-Venice train. This might seem surprising, given that she is also one of the main characters, but she belongs perhaps to that long line of fictional women (like Penelope, like Desdemona, like Dulcinea and so many others of less illustrious ancestry) whose existence is largely symbolic: they present the greatest danger to those who come into contact with them, as the narrator of *The Man of Feeling* seems to acknowledge: "For, as I well know," he says, "the most effective and lasting subjugations are based on pretence or, indeed, on something that has never existed." One wonders if the narrator meant to add: "or on something unfulfilled."

—Javier Marías, March 1987